IN PLAIN SIGHT

A SWEETS HIGH ROMANCE

AMY SPARLING

1
———

MADDIE

SPRING BREAK IS A DOUBLE-EDGED SWORD. On the one side, you get out of school for a total of nine days. Nine glorious days of sleeping as late as you want, wearing whatever you want, and spending time with family. Okay, most teenagers might not put the family part in the Spring Break Pros column, but I'm not like most teenagers. My little sisters, Emma and Starla, are my favorite people in the world. Emma starts kindergarten this year and Starla just turned two, so they're still young and adorable and generally, the best.

The downside of Spring Break? It's only a week to do all of those things. Then it's back to school for me, back to daycare for them, and the nightmare that is my life goes on as regularly scheduled.

Mom doesn't get a Spring Break. Vacations—paid or otherwise—aren't exactly in the Savings Mart vocabulary. The multi-million-dollar chain of grocery stories prefers to work their employees day in and day out, for very little pay and even less respect.

I take a deep breath and let my head rest against the window of school bus number forty-three. It's Friday, school is out, and I'm almost home. I don't know why I feel so bummed about life right now.

Spring Break . . . rah rah . . . woohoo.

Maybe it's because, no matter what Mom says about promising to give us a better life, I know it'll never happen. Maybe it's because we've spent four whole months here in Louetta, Texas and I haven't made a single friend. Unless I count Jacoby Anderson.

And I don't count Jacoby Anderson.

Ugh. We hit a pothole and my head bangs against the glass, making me wince. I sit up, then slouch down until my knees rest against the back of the seat in front of me. Jacoby is the only guy who's noticed me here at Sweets High School, and I have a pretty good idea that because of him, no other guy has noticed me since then.

We'd moved here just before Christmas because Mom finally got moved up to the top spot on the waiting list for our trailer house. The only rental within fifty miles of a Savings Mart that was only five hundred dollars a month rent. So we got the trailer, Mom rejoiced in cheaper bills, and I got to start at a new school.

Jacoby was in the office for disciplinary reasons, not that I knew it at the time, when I walked in on that first day to get my schedule. He offered to show me around, and he was cute —tall, dark skin and mesmerizing eyes—so of course I happily let him make me fifteen minutes late to first period because he was showing me around.

He asked me on a date that day, and I'd accepted. We went to the town's Christmas Festival of Lights, which is where they decorated the hell out of a park and made a super pretty and romantic pathway of lights to walk around while sipping hot chocolate.

I couldn't let him see where I lived, so I talked him into letting me meet him there.

It was a three mile walk in the cold, but it was worth it to shield him from the realities of my dirt poor life. We'd had a blast at first. He bought me hot chocolate and slung his arm around my shoulders while we walked. Everything was going pretty decent as far as first dates go, when I tripped over a wooden bridge and sprained my ankle.

There was no way I could walk home with my ankle swollen to the size of a softball. I had no choice. I had to let him drive me home.

I cringe just thinking of the memory.

I still remember the scowl on his face when I directed him to turn into the driveway that led to Quality Mobile Home Park—an epic offense of false advertising if you ask me. Immediately he was turned off by me in every aspect. I could just tell. But it only got worse when I told him which trailer was mine. Number four, the single-wide with faded paint and a sagging roof. There's also a piece of plywood covering a hole in the living room floor, that our landlord installed by duct taping around the edges to keep the roaches out, but Jacoby didn't need to know that. He was already grossed out enough.

"Please tell me you don't live here," he said.

"It's just temporary." Not exactly the truth, but it wasn't a lie either. We never stayed anywhere very long. Mom was always looking for cheaper rent.

He turned to me, lip cocked in disgust. "You know this is the pedophile house, right?"

I couldn't even feel the pain in my ankle anymore. I was so horrified that nothing else mattered. "No pedophiles live in my house, Jacoby. It's just my mom, my sisters, and me."

"No, he used to," he said. "It was on the news about a month ago. They busted this gross ass trashy man who had, like, kidnapped teenagers. He was already a sex offender but the trailer park let him move in any way because there are no schools around. Didn't you know that?"

I didn't know that. It never occurred to me to Google the address of wherever we were moving to. My stomach turned. "Well, no disgusting people live there now," I said.

"But how could you live in a trailer where kids were molested? That's just gross, Maddie."

I didn't really have an answer for him. After I'd gone inside and watched him back out of the driveway, tires peeling out onto the road like he couldn't get out of there fast enough, I never talked to him again. I barely even saw him at school, and our school isn't that big. It's like he decided I was the plague and found a way to inoculate himself against me.

The worst part? Mom didn't even care that we were living in a pedophile's old house. She just rolled her eyes and said he's in jail now and the house has been cleaned, so who cares?

I get off the bus when it stops on Market Street. Technically this is the stop for everyone who lives in an apartment complex right across the road, but I walk the extra half a mile home each day just so none of these idiots on my bus know where I live. I don't know why I even care. It's not like they talk to me.

Plus, I'm pretty sure the two stoners who sit in the back live in the same trailer park that I do, and they definitely don't care what people think of them.

The letters B and M are written on the inside of my list, a note I made this morning while I was getting the girls ready for daycare. Bread and Milk. We're out of both, and staples are just about the only thing my family eats each day.

Two weeks ago, Mom came home with a 12-count box of Pop Tarts that had been crushed by a forklift in the back of the store, and we all ate like freaking kings. Sugary, processed, name brand foods? It might as well have been Christmas.

I walk down Market Street to the gas station on the corner. Weird as it sounds, this place has the cheapest bread and milk, even cheaper than at Savings Mart. I grab one of each and take them to the register, where a woman who looks more like an old boxer than a lady rings me up.

"Four seventy-two, darlin'."

I swipe the debit card I share with Mom. The machine beeps twice, this low and aggravating sound that totally gives it away, like it's shouting THIS PERSON IS POOR to everyone in the freaking store.

"It's declined, honey. You got another card?"

No I don't have another card. I'm seventeen, and Mom's

credit is so shot even loan sharks won't lend her a dime. This bank account is all we have.

"Um, I don't think so." Heat rushes to my cheeks. Nothing is worse than having your card declined in a store. Except maybe being told you live in a pedophile house by a really cute guy.

"Sorry, can you just cancel it?" I say, my throat dry. "I'll go put them back on the shelf."

The cashier, Judy according to her name tag, gives me this tight-lipped frown, which makes her wrinkly face even more wrinkly.

"You come in here a lot," she says, eyeing me.

"Yes, ma'am?" I say, not sure if I'm supposed to answer that.

"You always buy bread and milk." Again, not really a question, but I feel compelled to reply.

I lift my shoulders. "This store is the cheapest for those things."

"The boss thinks low grocery prices will bring in more people who blow all their money on lottery tickets," she says with a nod. "I think it works."

A guy walks up behind me now, a case of beer and a pack of peanuts in his hands. I don't know what I'm supposed to do now. I can't pay, I'm trying to leave, but she won't stop talking to me.

My heart speeds up, and then Judy reaches under the counter and opens an old wallet. She takes out a five-dollar bill and then punches it into the cash register.

"It's on me today, kiddo. You have a good day."

"Really? Um, wow thanks." I'm mumbling, but Judy's creased lips turn up in a smile.

"You can pay it forward someday when you're able."

"I will, thank you," I say, grabbing the bags and giving her my most grateful smile. It feels wrong and a little icky to accept a stranger's money like that, but there was a guy standing behind me, and I didn't want to make a scene. Plus. My sisters really need this food. I don't know why my mom refuses to sign up for government assistance. Food stamps would go a long way for situations like this, when our bank account is no doubt in the negative.

I should really try to find a job. Mom doesn't think it's feasible for me to work too since I'm the main babysitter when the girls aren't at daycare, but maybe I can work something out. Maybe I can find some way to earn a little cash to help us get by.

With that idea in mind, I walk down the strip of stores on Market Street, choosing to go inside an ice cream shop to see if they're hiring.

As soon as I walk in, a rush of refrigerated air and the scent of expensive perfume hits me. Three girls talk animatedly while they lean over the glass counter, looking for an ice cream flavor. It's the M's, I know it just from seeing the back of them.

The three most popular girls in school, all with a name that starts with an M. It's kind of like me, only my name is the only thing we have in common. They are all beautiful, filthy rich, and always seem to smell nice.

These girls haven't worked a day in their life and they're very proud of that. Must be nice.

I walk up to the counter and ask the girl if they're hiring. She's only about my age, maybe even a year younger, and she frowns. "I don't think so. I could ask my boss though?"

Suddenly I feel too suffocated to linger around anymore. "No thanks, that's fine."

My phone rings and I dig it out of my backpack.

"Oh my god, is that a flip phone?" one of the M's says, her smoky eyes bursting open wide. "Like, who even has those anymore?"

"I didn't even know they would still work," another one says.

I don't bother meeting their critical gazes as I answer the call and push my way back out the door and into the safety of the sidewalk.

"Hey, Mom," I say, letting out a breath I didn't realize I was holding.

"Where are you? You should have been home by now?"

"I was getting milk and bread," I say, deciding not to tell her about Judy's charity. Mom no doubt already knows the account is negative. "We're out."

"Ugh, honey, we don't need any of that," Mom says, sounding like she's in a rush.

"Yes we definitely do," I say. "It's Spring Break and I'm watching the girls all week, remember?"

If they don't go to daycare for the week, we get to save money. But they still need to be fed.

"Honey, just come home and hurry. I have a big surprise for you."

"What kind of surprise?" I say, not bothering to pick up

the pace. Maybe it's another box of crushed food from her work. That would be a lifesaver right about now.

"The best surprise of your entire life," Mom says.

Something in her voice sends chills down my spine. Mom's not one to exaggerate the truth, and she's never sounded so happy, not in my entire life.

"Okay," I say, walking a little faster. "This better be good."

"Trust me, Maddie. It is."

2

———

COLBY

THE BEAMER'S engine roars to life, sounding like it's excited for Spring Break too, even though it's just a car. I crank the air conditioning and lean back in the black leather seat, closing my eyes to just chill for a minute. Midterms kicked my ass this semester, and I can only imagine how bad finals will be. I feel like I'll need this entire week off school just to recuperate from all the studying I did for these stupid tests. Of course, taking a course load of four AP classes at once never bothered my brother Greg, so I won't let anyone know it bothers me

I let out a deep breath and crank the radio. It's Spring Break, after all. Hell yeah. I pull out of the school parking lot, letting my car speed away from that hell hole as fast as I can legally go. Which isn't fast, because I'm still in a school zone.

Josh calls me, and I answer the phone on my car's Bluetooth speaker because God knows I can't afford another ticket for talking on the phone. At least this way, any passing cops will think I'm just talking to myself.

"Sup, man?"

"The Getaway tonight," Josh says. In the background I can hear the roar of his old Camaro, a classic '76 that he borrows from his dad every so often to drive to school and look like a badass. "Bryce is meeting at my house, so you wanna just pick us up, say around seven?"

"The Getaway?" I say with a groan. "Come on, man. Anywhere but there."

"Getaway freaking rules, dude. Just have your ass here by seven, okay?"

The call ends and I roll my eyes as I turn toward my neighborhood. The Getaway is located in what used to be a clothing store before the company went bankrupt. It's described as a "club for teens" and yes, it's exactly as lame as it sounds. There's dancing, a DJ, arcade games, and a bar that serves food and non-alcoholic drinks. So it's pretty much like a nightclub, but for people who can't buy alcohol. Without alcohol, I really don't see a reason for grinding up against strangers under the blinking of multi-colored lights to some crappy pop music, but it is what it is. My friends love it.

And at least there's a ton of girls there, so I guess that partially makes up for the whole lame factor. Given the choice, I'd rather binge watch Netflix in my room with a large cheese pizza, but the guys won't go for that.

Plus, there are girls. And I could really use a girl right about now.

I don't mean that literally. I don't *use* girls. I treat them with the respect they deserve, just like my mother taught me. It's too bad that respect thing doesn't go both ways. If I had a dollar for every time I was approached by a girl who only wanted the popularity that comes with dating a member of the football team, I'd be so freaking rich I could buy my own private jet and get the hell out of his small ass town.

I *love* the idea of having a girlfriend. But every girl around here sucks. They spend more time bragging about dating me on social media than they do, ya know, actually dating me. They want me to buy them things, take them places, do all of the gold-digging things their heart desires, but when I was in the hospital having surgery on my knee, who came to visit me?

None of them, that's for sure.

With bitter anger and spite flowing through my veins, I make it home and head straight for the shower. I still have a few hours before I need to be a Josh's but I need some time to myself right now. A hot shower, an hour of watching TV, and maybe a snack. Maybe that will help me decompress. I mean, having a girlfriend isn't the only thing in the world to care about.

But what can I say? I want one.

I want to love and laugh and hang out with a pretty girl who cares about me just as much as I care about her. I want secret inside jokes and late nights on the phone and lingering goodbyes on her doorstep.

Sometimes I think I need to start an entirely new life on a whole different planet in order to have the opportunity to meet someone who could share these things with me. Living in Greg Jensen's shadow has kind of ruined me, socially.

My older brother was a rock star athlete, a God with the ladies, and graduated top of his class five years ago. And apparently, just because I look like him and share his DNA, everyone expects the same of me.

I did my share of being a playboy womanizer in sophomore and junior year, but it got old fast. That's not really me. Maybe that's why my senior year sucks.

When I've steamed up the shower and used nearly all the hot water, I step out, wrap a towel around my waist and reach for my deodorant.

Only it's empty, so I toss it in the trash and head out in the hallway to grab another tube from the stash my dad keeps in his bathroom. Shouting and passive aggressive comments fly out of my parent's room, as loud as if the door wasn't shut.

I stop in the hallway, sighing, as I listen to them go on and on, arguing about money. It's always about money.

My parents love each other, they really do. But they are awful when it comes to budgeting. And that doesn't make any sense because they're both accountants. Go figure.

Deciding I can probably just chill on my bed for a while without deodorant, I turn and head back to my room.

My parent's door flies open, and Dad calls out, "Maybe if you took one less trip to the ed salon every month, we could afford the house insurance."

"You love my hair and you know it, John," Mom calls back.

I roll my eyes. They both have a point. The thing with my parents is that although they're madly in love, they also have quite a "keeping up with the Jones's" complex that leaves them perpetually broke. They love living the good life, even when we can't afford it.

"Colby," Dad says, making me freeze in place just before the safety of my bedroom.

I turn around. "Hey, Dad, what's up?"

"I can't give you any money tonight," he says staring at me like I was just about to ask him for a few hundred. (I wasn't, by the way.)

"That's fine, I'm good."

Dad looks at me the vein in his forehead protruding, but finally he shrugs. "Good."

3

____

MADDIE

SOMETHING IS weird at the trailer park. I can tell even when I'm still half a block away. A large moving truck is parked in the road that divides both rows of mobile homes. No one who lives in one of these places can afford a moving truck. Maybe it's really the police and they're here to seize a trailer full of drugs or something. But I don't see any cop cars, no flashing red and blue lights—which is actually ironic because here at Quality Mobile Home Park, there's usually one set of flashing lights once a day.

I walk into the faded gates that surround the property of run down mobile homes in an effort to shield the public from the crap hole that it is, and then narrow my eyes. It really looks like that moving truck is parked next to our trailer. But it can't be for us because two muscular men in white tank tops and jeans walk down the ramp on the back of the truck. Only Mom, me, and my sisters live in our house.

I watch them as I get closer to my house. One of the men walks back carrying a pink dollhouse. It was on sale for five dollars at the Goodwill last year and I got it for Emma for Christmas.

Okay, this is not good.

Are we being evicted?

Or . . . *robbed?*

Just when curiosity is getting the better of me, Mom appears, telling the second man to make sure the mirror from her antique vanity set isn't scratched.

"Mom?" I say, stopping on the gravel road a few feet before our driveway. "What's going on?"

Mom turns to me, grinning so big you can see her crooked teeth. Teeth notwithstanding, Rose Sinclair is incredibly beautiful, especially for a woman in her early forties. She has long medium brown hair and big brown eyes. Even though we've always been poor, Mom never skimps on skin care, always moisturizing and cleansing, saying your skin is what shows age, so it's best to take care of it.

She smells like baby powder lotion even now as she engulfs me in a hug.

"Surprise!" Her big eyes sparkle as she pulls back, holding me tightly by the shoulders. "We're getting the hell out of this place!"

Okay, three things cross my mind all at once:

---

1. How the hell did she find a cheaper place to rent than here?

2. How much worse will it be than this falling-down trailer?

3. Oh well, at least I get to move schools and
forget all about how much Jacoby humiliated me.

———————

"Okay," I say instead of voicing any of my thoughts. Then, because I can't help myself, I follow it up with, "Why?"

Mom gnaws on her bottom lip, a strand of hair falling from the messy bun on top of her head. She takes a deep breath and holds up her hand, palm facing herself. "This is why!"

It's only four in the afternoon, so the sun is still shining pretty brightly. That's why I nearly go blind in the seconds that follow.

Then my jaw drops. Mom's wearing a diamond ring the size of a freaking Ring Pop. (Okay, maybe not that big, but the thing sure is shining like the North Star.)

"What the hell is that?"

Mom frowns, causing a tiny splash of wrinkles around her lips. "Honey, language."

"Sorry," I say rolling my eyes. "What the *heck* is that? Did you rob a jewelry store? Are we jewel thieves now? Hmm . . . I guess I could get behind that," I say, sarcastically putting a finger to my lips like I'm thinking it over.

Mom laughs. "You are hilarious, Maddie. No, this is an engagement ring. Landon proposed to me!"

She looks so genuinely, unbelievably, happy. Her eyes sparkle as much as her behemoth of a ring, and she seems ten years younger. She's also staring at me like she expects me to be just as excited.

"Landon?" I say, lifting a brow. "Is that the guy you've been dating?"

"Yes, silly." Now she rolls her eyes. The moving men keep walking past us, going into the house and then returning with boxes of our stuff. "You know Landon. I've been dating him since we moved here."

"No, Mom. I don't know Landon. I know *of* Landon."

Ever since my dad left Mom in their senior year of college when I was just a baby, and then Emma's dad left Mom when Emma was just a baby, and then Starla's dad left mom—well, the moment he found out she was pregnant—Mom has instituted a strict rule. No introducing the men she dates to her kids until she's positive it'll work out.

Needless to say, in the two and a half years since Starla has been born, we haven't met a single guy.

I know it sounds like Mom maybe isn't the greatest person, but she is. She's loving and kind and she cares so much it tends to ruin her. She's just made a few bad mistakes in life, and when you add them all together it makes her seem like trailer trash single mom of three.

I *hate* that so much. My mom is such a great person and she doesn't deserve that title. It's not like she's some inept drug addict. She's not a prostitute and she refuses to get on welfare, no matter how much I might ask her to. Things are tight, and Mom deals with it in her own way.

Like how five years ago when my real dad—a man named Stephan who only went to college because his parents made him—found us and apologized for not being there, Mom wasn't mean to him. She let him in my life, saying I need a real dad if he wants to be one. It was awkward as hell, but he apologized for never being there, gave me a check for five thousand dollars, and then slowly stopped calling over the course of a few weeks.

Mom insisted that I keep the money for myself, but I knew we were two months behind on rent and Mom's knees were killing her from walking to work every day. So I paid the rent and bought her a car. A bad mom would have just kept the money for herself.

My mom is not a bad mom.

Which is why I'm staring at her like she's lost her mind. "A guy you've known four months proposed to you and now we're moving. Am I getting that right?"

"Yes, honey." Mom's smile flattens, and a little crease appears in her forehead. "Look, I know it seems sudden, but it's not for me. I knew the moment I met him that I wanted to be with him forever. And I should have introduced you girls to him a lot sooner, I should have. Then this wouldn't be so weird."

"Where are we moving?" I ask, trying to give her the benefit of the doubt.

"To his house. It's *our* house now, honey. And guess what? Everyone gets their own room!"

I narrow my eyes. That does sound great . . . "Does he have any kids?"

"Nope," she says shaking her head. "But he loves kids and he's always wanted them. He's going to love you guys."

"What if he doesn't?" I ask, crossing my arms. "What if he *thinks* he likes kids but then Starla has one of her epic meltdowns and he realizes he hates kids and wants us to leave? How will get find another cheap place to live?"

"Maddie, that won't happen," Mom says, reaching for my hand. She squeezes it, her skin warm against mine. "I know this is sudden, but it's the best thing that ever happened to us. Landon is the best thing that's ever happened to me. I swear to you."

A knot is slowly forming itself in my stomach, and about a million alarm bells are going off in my head. What if this Landon guy is a serial murderer who just lured in his next victims? Or worse? *We haven't even met him!*

I close my eyes and take a deep breath, letting it out slowly. "Where are the girls?"

"They're still at daycare. They can stay there until six, so we're hoping to have their rooms unpacked by then. I read in a parenting magazine at work that when you move with kids, their rooms should be the last to be packed up and the first to be unpacked."

I resist the urge to roll my eyes, I really do. "Okay, well don't put them in separate rooms."

Mom's brows furrow. "Why not?"

"Because they've been together their whole lives. Put them together and let them choose for themselves if they want to separate later on. It'll help them transition to some strange new house."

"I guess that's a good idea," Mom says. "Let me go tell the movers."

Okay, so as weird and insane as this day is, I am starting to get a little excited. I mean, the pedophile house is gross. There are roaches that skitter across the floor when you turn on the lights, a piece of plywood duct taped to the floor, and every single window leaks when it rains. It always smells like mold and I've had more than one nightmare that the roof will suddenly collapse, killing us all.

If Landon has a house—a *real* house—this could be a good thing.

I could get a good night's rest without hearing the cops arresting some idiot a few trailers down. I could turn on the lights without worrying about roaches.

Yes, I decide, telling that knot in my chest to go away. *This could be a good thing.*

4

—————

COLBY

THE ARGUING CONTINUES in the kitchen, although I hear Mom laugh a few times, so I guess they're slowly going back to normal. The thing is, my parents both hate being broke, but they both also love to spend all of their money. It doesn't take a financial genius to know that'll never work out in the long run.

Last time Greg was visiting from Rice University, he gave me a long lecture on how we need to make sure we get a good education and a high-paying job because we'll be the ones who need to take care of them when we're older. I don't exactly like the idea of finally growing up, having my own family, and then moving my parents into the back room. Maybe the wonder child Greg will take care of that for me.

Back in my room, I flip on the TV and settle into my bed, trying to get some of that relaxing in before what I know will be an annoying night out. The Getaway is literally the stupidest place in town and I have no idea why every senior at RCHS is freaking obsessed with it. Yeah, sometimes it's kinda hot watching the girls pretend to be drunk and dance on the bar, but mostly it just makes me feel bad for them.

An hour later, when my show is over and I've sadly reached the end of the newest season, something dawns on me. Dad said he can't give me any money, which means he probably won't have money for the rest of the week. I've got about fifty bucks in my wallet, and the entrance fee at The Getaway is ten. Add in the food and non-alcoholic drinks and I'll be nearly broke after tonight.

Trust me, I hate getting money from my parents, but they refuse to let me get a job, no matter how badly I want one. Dad thinks it's a sign that he's not a good provider if his kids work, and Mom thinks I should focus on school. Being in all AP classes with a straight A average just isn't good enough, I guess.

With a sigh, I reach for my phone and call Josh.

"Dude, let's go somewhere else tonight," I say. "Somewhere free."

"I feel ya," Josh says. He does get to work because his parents aren't as well-off, so money means more to him than to the rest of my friends. "What about the beach? I hear there's gonna be a bonfire tonight."

The beach is an hour's drive away, but it's Spring Break so it'll be packed. With girls who *don't* pretend to be drunk and dance on bars.

"Sounds good," I say. "But you're pitching in for gas."

"Deal. Come get us."

Bryce lives down the street from Josh, so he's already waiting there when I arrive, a case of Bud Light in his hand. Together, these two idiots are my best friends, but Josh and I are the closest. Bryce disappears a few weeks at a time when he gets a new girlfriend. Luckily for us, they never stick around very long, and he's back to stealing beer from his parent's massive stockpile in the rec room.

"Spring BREAAAAK," Bryce says, followed by a whoop as he piles into the back seat of my BMW. He sets the case of beer in the seat next to him, then buckles it in, saying, "Precious cargo," when I lift an eyebrow at him.

I jam out to the radio while the guys argue about whether PlayStation or Xbox is the greatest gaming console ever invented, and by the time we get to the beach, they still haven't come to a conclusion.

The sun is still up, so the bonfire hasn't started yet, but in the distance I can see the pyramid-shaped stack of logs waiting to be lit. The beach is definitely busier than usual for Spring Break, and a ton of vehicles are parked on the sand, tents set up and grills cooking mouth-watering food. Too bad we only have beer because now I'm starving.

We find some guys from the football team who have already lit their own bonfire, although this one is a small, personal size. I actually like these better than the huge ones. You can roast marshmallows on them. Billy, a junior linebacker who is always stuffing his mouth, brought a crap ton of s'mores ingredients, and he invites me to have some.

I sit next to him, making s'mores and drinking a beer, and gazing out at the hot ass college girls running into the water. Josh and Bryce are still arguing like idiots over the video game thing, although the number of girls in skimpy bikinis are starting to win over their attention.

I'm not delusional enough to think I'd ever find the future

love of my life at a bonfire on the beach, but that doesn't stop me from imagining it. And I know for a fact that if I were to mention this to the guys, they'd rag on me until I die from embarrassment.

So I take another sip of beer, eat another s'more, and just chill.

"Hey there," a sultry voice calls out a while later.

I know the voice before I see her face, and maybe that's why I take a while to look over. "Sup."

Maria recently cut all her hair off into a short bob, but her insanely drastic cat-eye eyeliner is still the same. She looks good, and she smells good, as she sidles up to me, inching between me and the bonfire with her ass right in my face until she gets to the empty chair next to me.

I know better than to give her any of my time. Her dad owns Blue Star beer bottling company—like, the *entire* company—and she's been treated like a princess her entire life. I am pretty certain that no teenage guy on the planet is capable of treating her as well as she expects from all of the peasants she considers below her station in life.

I made the very big mistake of getting drunk and making out with her on this very beach last summer, and it took me three months to shake her off. The girl is a big fan of the long, super dramatic text message that tries to make you feel like crap for rejecting her. Why she's even interested in me when I live in Shady Grove, and she lives on a two-hundred-acre ranch with a mansion of a house, is beyond me. The girl's dad is friends with *celebrities*. They are literally the jet-setters of Louetta, Texas.

And now she's snaking her slender fingers up my thigh.

"Colby, why are you ignoring me?" she whines, tilting a pouty face in my direction.

I shove another marshmallow on my metal stick and point it toward the fire. "I'm not ignoring you. I asked what's up."

"No, you said 'sup', and that's not nearly the same thing." She leans over, resting her elbow on the arm of my lawn chair. She smells like a fruity perfume mixed with sunblock. I look over and she licks her lips, her ample boobs practically spilling out of the pink scrap of fabric she calls a swimsuit.

"What do you want with me?" I say.

"I want the famous Jensen treatment," she says, winking.

I heave a sigh and stare at my marshmallow, which is now on fire. My brother Greg has somewhat of a . . . reputation . . . when it comes to pleasing girls in bed. And because of this, everyone thinks I have it, too.

Like Greg called me aside one day and said, "Brother, let me teach you how to be a sex god" or something.

Trust me, he never did.

"What?" I say, playing dumb. "You want me to make you a s'more?"

She rolls her eyes. Stands up. "I don't make this offer to anyone, *Colby*. You should really stop playing whatever game this is."

She walks in front of me again, leaning down low so her boobs are in my face, her lips touching my ear. "You know you want me."

Her breath is warm and it smells like tequila. A million rude things to say come to my head but instead I check the time on my cell phone, pretending like her words didn't mean anything to me.

She scoffs and saunters off, her feet leaving a trail in the sand.

"Dude," Billy says, coming back from the ice chest with two new beers. "That chick is hot."

"Yeah," I say, rubbing my eyebrow. I can still remember her text messages and how they wouldn't stop until I wrote her back. "But she's not worth it."

5

———

MADDIE

I LOVE DRIVING. There's something about being behind the wheel, knowing I'm in control of where the car takes me, that I find really comforting. We only have the one car that I'd bought with my biological dad's guilt money, and Mom insists that I take it to pick up the girls from daycare. She says she's going to ride with the movers to our new house and get everything set up for when the girls arrive.

She also gave me a twenty-dollar bill—something insanely valuable in our household—and told me to get the ice cream first so she has time to get ready for the big house reveal.

I leave the windows rolled down as I drive toward the daycare, occasionally glancing at the ripped off piece of paper with Landon's address on it. I guess it's our new address too, but that's a little hard to accept right now.

4848 Pinegrove Lane

Louetta, Texas

It's so weird. I can't recall a time we've ever had an

address without an apartment or unit number behind the street name. An entire house. A *real* house, with a yard and a driveway all to ourselves. This is a pretty big deal, but we still don't even know Landon, so I can only imagine how awkward this entire thing will be.

When I arrive at Little Texans' Daycare, my heart gets all excited at the idea of seeing the girls. My little sisters are my life, and pretty much my best friends. I don't really care how dorky that sounds. I know sometimes Mom feels bad about it because the girls run to me when they're scared or happy or need someone to talk to. It's not Mom's fault they're closer to me. Mom's been working her ass off ever since they were born, so many of the parenting tasks have fallen to me over the years.

I wonder if that's going to change now that we're moving in with Landon. If Mom doesn't need as much money to pay the bills, maybe she can cut back on her work hours. She can definitely lose her second job waiting tables part-time in the middle of the night. This thought alone makes me happy. Mom deserves a break. She also deserves a man who truly loves her. I hope Landon is that man.

I take a deep breath and shake away the nerves in the pit of my stomach. The girls will be relying on me to show them how to feel about this new move, so I need to keep a straight face and act like people do this all the time. Hell, maybe they do. I wouldn't know.

The daycare smells like Lysol and diapers, a scent that's almost a little overwhelming until you get used to it. Emma notices me first. She's laying on a colorful carpet in front of an old TV where they still play VHS Disney movies in the afternoons.

"Maddie!" she says, jumping to her feet. "I made you something!" She runs over to her cubby, where she grabs her blanket and a piece of construction paper that's about the size of a postcard.

"Why are you so late today?" she asks, frowning up at me. Emma is very thin for her age, with silky blond hair and blue eyes, all traits of which she got from her dad. He was nice enough, giving me Christmas presents for the two years he was dating Mom. But he left, just like they always do.

"Well, we have a surprise for you," I tell her, ruffling her hair as she hands me the construction paper. It's colored like a stained glass window, where she pressed really hard with her Crayons to make the colors silky on the paper.

"This is beautiful, Em. Thank you."

She grins up at me, all toothy and wise beyond her four and a half years. "Is it a good surprise?" she asks.

"Yes," I say, taking her hand and waving at the older lady who's sitting next to the TV. We walk down the hallway to where the toddlers are kept in a room that's filled with toys and even more of that diaper smell.

"Are we moving again?" Emma asks.

I give her this playful look. "Maybe . . ."

"Good, because I hate our house," she says, wrinkling her nose. "Is the new house better?"

"I think so," I say, giving her an unsure smile.

When we get to the toddler room, Starla sees me and lights up, throwing her handful of toys right to the floor as she waddles over to me, something that looks like peas staining her onesie.

Her caretaker, Mrs. Heather, waves at me while looking at her phone. "See you tomorrow."

I pick up Starla and we head out to the car. The girls are always excited to see me, but when I pull into the Sonic parking lot and announce that Mom has given us money for ice cream, they erupt into screams and giggles.

We all order a hot fudge sundae, even though I know Starla will make a mess with hers since she's only two years old. It doesn't matter; we're celebrating after all.

Whatever house Landon lives in; I am pretty positive it doesn't have a big hole in the floor that's covered with plywood.

We jam out to some music on the radio, and after a few moments of reveling in the very rare treat of ice cream, Emma calls my name. Her lips are covered in hot fudge and I'm sure her hands are sticky and gross by now, too.

"Yes, ma'am?" I say, looking back at her in the backseat.

"Are you going to tell Starla the secret?"

"Do you think I should?" I ask.

She nods eagerly, ice cream sliding off her plastic spoon.

"Hey, Starla," I say, twisting in my seat to see her.

Starla looks up from her ice cream, which is mostly all over her face as well.

"We're getting a new house today!" I say in my most excited kid voice.

Starla looks at me and then back at her ice cream. "Kay!"

Emma laughs. "I don't think she gets it," she says.

"Probably not," I say, shaking my head.

When we're finished eating and we've wasted a good hour in the Sonic parking lot, I decide it's probably late enough to head to our new house.

Taking the paper, I type the address into the GPS unit in our car. It thinks for a second and then shows the destination.

I lift an eyebrow. That can't be right. 4848 Pinegrove Lane is showing up as being in Shady Heights.

Frowning, I reset the address and try again. It takes me to the same location. My blood runs cold.

Shady Heights?

As in, the neighborhood with signs advertising that the homes start from $600,000?

No. Freaking. Way.

I call Mom and she answers on the first ring. "I just need to confirm the address you gave me is right," I say, trying to focus when a million things are running through my head.

"Yep, that's right," Mom says after telling me the address again.

"That's in Shady Heights."

She laughs. "Surprise!"

I swallow the lump in my throat and stare at the GPS screen. Not only is Shady Heights the richest subdivision in the county, it's also still in the RCHS school district, meaning I won't be changing schools after all.

"Shady Heights," I whisper to myself after I've ended the call with Mom. I put the car in reverse and then start heading that way, my mind going in a million directions at once.

I never in my life thought I'd ever step foot inside a house in that neighborhood.

And now I'm going to live there.

6

COLBY

THIS MIGHT BE the worst Spring Break ever. It's as if the moment I realized I didn't want to be my brother, everything in the universe decided to work against me out of spite. Even my parents seem to like me a little less with each thing I do that doesn't fit on their agenda for my future. They're my parents and I love them and all, but they can't just force me into a mold of something I don't want to be.

After the uneventful beach party, I'd driven home feeling miserable and wishing I'd gotten drunk. Then of course, I'd have had to spend the night at the beach, which would have made for a worse night. So I guess staying sober and getting home was a good thing.

But now that I'm here, it's three in the morning and I can't sleep. Senior year is supposed to be the year you glide through school, knowing what your future holds and being old enough to forget about all the lame crap that happens in younger grades. Instead, I feel like I'm stuck spinning my wheels, moving in no direction at all.

Except maybe down.

I lay on my back in bed, tossing a foam ball up in the air and catching it over and over again. I've spent a lot of time in this bed, not sleeping. Just after football season started, I injured my knee and had to have two surgeries. After the first surgery, my parents and doctors were hopeful that I'd play sports again and attract a scout for college football.

The very thought made me cringe. It's bad enough that I've been hiking balls and passing balls and playing football since I was in fifth grade—but now they wanted me to play in college, too?

The first surgery didn't help much, and my injury was worse than ever. The second surgery helped a lot, but I was given a warning that another injury from football could leave me in a wheelchair, and my parents regretfully let me quit the team. I'm still technically "on" the team since I was at the start of the school year, but I'm benched, there for moral support of my teammates only.

Honestly? I couldn't be happier.

I don't want to play football. It's not that the game isn't fun, it's that Greg played football. Greg got a scholarship. Greg played college ball. Greg is the greatest son on earth. I get it.

I don't want to be Greg.

My stomach rumbles and I toss the ball into a pile of dirty clothes on the floor. All those s'mores for dinner didn't really do the trick. I need protein. No, I need cheese and pasta—even better.

Being as quiet as possible because my parents are asleep, I head into the kitchen and set a pot of water on the stove to boil. I dig out some elbow macaroni and begin grating all three of the types of cheese we have in the fridge. I decide to fry up some bacon while I'm at it, working quickly while my stomach growls, begging for me to hurry up.

The only thing better than homemade mac and cheese is adding chopped up bacon to it.

I eat what's probably five servings of pasta while watching Netflix. Though my body is tired, my brain doesn't feel like sleeping, and that blows. This comfort food really puts me in a better mood though, and I find myself thinking not for the first time that it would be fun to go to culinary school. I love cooking almost as much as I love eating. Maybe I could own a restaurant one day.

That would really piss off my parents, who'd like to see me become an accountant like them or something they consider better, like a lawyer or even a doctor. But if it's my future, I should be excited about it, right?

I'd like to work for myself, I know that much. Having a little bistro or steakhouse in town would be kind of awesome. I could work on signature dishes and have a goal of attracting the attention of one of those Food TV shows that travel around doing stories on awesome restaurants.

I'm imagining myself on TV when my phone beeps with a new Snapchat alert.

It's from Maria. She's wearing black underwear and a hot pink bra, posing in front of a tall mirror in a way that shows off all her curves.

The photo caption says, *I miss you* and I realize one second too late that since I opened the thing, she'll know I'm awake too.

Two minutes later, another snap comes through and I groan, hating myself for being so stupid. This one is a selfie, up close with her boobs squished together between her arms.

Talk to me the caption says.

I debate what to write back. Then I realize I don't have to write back. Sure, the app tells her I've seen her provocative pictures, but it doesn't force me to reply to her, or to even react at all. I let the snap expire and then toss my phone on the pillow next to me. Maybe ignoring her will finally teach her that I'm not interested. She, and so many girls like her, seem to think that showing off their goods will make guys come running into their arms. I don't want a girl like that, one who shows off everything she has to any ol' guy who comes around. My dream girl wouldn't act like that.

Unfortunately, just like my restaurant idea, my dream girl exists somewhere only in my imagination.

7

MADDIE

I WAKE up on Saturday morning to the scent of lavender bedsheets and the soft glow of sunlight streaming in through the window. Only my window is covered in newspapers to keep out the heat and my room always smells like mold. So what the heck is going on?

My eyes fling open, staring at an immaculate white ceiling. All of the events of yesterday come back to me, nearly knocking the breath out of my lungs. It almost felt like moving into our new home was some kind of dream, some fantastic illusion that would never actually happen in my lifetime.

Yet, as I scoot up in my new bed, letting my head rest against the padded headboard, the feather down comforter soft under my fingertips, I realize it did happen. This is my new room.

This mansion, this two story gigantic house with six bedrooms, two kitchens, three living areas, a movie room and a swimming pool—it's all my new home.

Last night was a whirlwind of awesome. My little sisters were in awe as we drove up to the house, which has an actual gate in the front and everything. Mom was watching for us and she opened the gate when we arrived. Landon later gave me a gate key to keep in my car to open it myself.

First impressions of Landon are pretty good. He's a little older than Mom, with salt and pepper hair that looks good on him. He's tall, handsome (for a guy in his forties), and very smart. He's the kind of guy who uses words like *ergo* and *fiduciary* in his everyday conversations.

He'd said he was an investment banker and although I'm not exactly sure what that is, it's clear he makes a lot of money from it. And the best part is that he seems to really love Mom. They held hands all night long, smiled at each other constantly and laughed about everything.

Mom is like a freaking teenager, she's so in love with him. I think this upcoming marriage might be a good thing, for all of us, so long as they're really in love. And it seems like they are.

Starla was super shy around Landon, but Emma warmed up to him quickly, especially after he showed the girls to their new room. Mom had taken my advice and put their stuff into one room to share for now. In a house where the hallways are bigger than our old trailer, I don't think they'd know what to do with two rooms.

Their old mattress that used to be on the floor is in the trash now. It's been replaced with a brand new set of bedroom furniture that Mom and Landon picked out. It's white, curved on the edges and looks fit for a princess.

There's a matching set in the room across the hall, waiting for when the girls decide to have separate rooms.

My room is also furnished. I have a black queen-sized bed with a white padded headboard. The dresser and vanity are beautiful and totally empty. I can't really bring myself to unpack my crappy clothes into something so nice.

Landon and Mom told me to choose any of the rooms I wanted, but I picked the one next door to the girls' room so I'd be close to them. The furniture was already here, and although Landon keeps saying I can change it out with other furniture in the other guest rooms, or even buy new stuff if I want, I've assured him this is fine.

I have a bay window that looks out into the front yard, shimmery lavender curtains with little sparrows on them, and a plush lavender rug on top of the already plush and heavenly white carpet. We've never lived anywhere with carpet that wasn't covered in stains and grossness. Now, I could stand here forever, letting my toes thread through the soft fibers.

Everything is amazing. I feel like I've stepped out of the real world and into a dream where I don't ever want to wake up.

Last night was such a whirlwind, that after Landon took us out to dinner at a fancy steakhouse where the meals were so expensive the prices weren't listed on the menu, we got home with only enough time to get a shower and go to bed.

Today, I've been promised a tour of the place, and I'm most excited about the pool and the movie room. I mean, he can't really have a theater in his house, can he?

My door swings open and Emma and Starla appear,

holding hands and grinning. "I found your room," Emma says.

"I told you I was just right next door," I tell her with a laugh. Normally, it takes ages to get the girls to go to bed, but after our night last night, they fell fast asleep in their new beds—a twin for Emma and a crib for Starla—without so much as a fight. Starla rubs at her sleepy eyes and then rushes up to me. I pull them onto my bed, which has a mattress so plush it's like three feet off the floor. The girls lay on my bed and Starla starts sucking her thumb, a sure sign that she's content here.

"I'm hungry," Emma says, squishing my comforter between her fingers. "How do we get food?"

"How about we venture down to the kitchen together, hmm?" I say. Honestly, I'm not really sure how to get down there, and I have no idea where Mom's bedroom is, but she'd said their room is on the first floor while ours is upstairs.

There's a light tap on the door and I startle at the sight of a strange woman standing there.

"Good morning, Miss Maddie," she says, smiling sweetly as she enters my room. She's about fifty years old I guess, wearing a light blue dress and white shoes. It should really dawn on me before she says it, but I'm a little flustered as of late.

"I'm Pamela, your maid. It's so nice to meet you."

Maid?

"Um, hi," I say, sitting up straighter in bed. "This is Emma and Starla."

She smiles and nods at the girls. "Breakfast is almost ready, would you like me to take you down?"

"Oh, that would be great," I say, throwing off the blankets. I'm wearing leggings and a T-shirt and am suddenly very grateful I didn't sleep in my underwear like I usually do when it's too hot outside and Mom doesn't want to run the air conditioner because it's expensive.

Pamela tells me I can call her Pam, and she leads us down the ornate staircase and around a few corners and hallways until we reach the kitchen, where the smell of bacon and syrup makes my mouth water.

Mom and Landon sit at the kitchen table, drinking coffee and talking excitedly. The way she looks at her new fiancé makes her look so much younger, so less stressed out. Seeing her so happy makes that constant knot in my chest seems to fade away.

There's another stranger manning the stove, a man with dark hair and a tattoo of a pepper mill on his forearm. He gives me a polite nod, then loads up a platter with strips of bacon. Landon has a freaking personal chef.

"Good morning, girls!" Mom says, rising from her chair and rushing over to us. "You hungry?"

We all nod, and Mom puts Stella into a high chair, one of the expensive kinds unlike the thrift store one we used to have.

"Good morning, Landon," I say, smiling politely.

"Morning," he says, setting down his paper. Yes, he reads the paper at the kitchen table. How posh. "Did you sleep well?"

"Probably better than I've ever slept in my life," I say, meaning every word.

We're served breakfast by our own personal chef—whose

name is Marc. I drink a ton of fresh squeezed orange juice and eat more bacon than I've ever had in one sitting.

I can tell my sisters are enjoying the abundance of food just as much as I am, because their little hands are sticky with syrup and they can't stop smiling. This wonderful breakfast probably contains more food than we used to have in an entire week.

"So, Maddie," Mom says, stirring her coffee. "I was thinking we could go shopping today. Maybe get some new clothes and some stuff to decorate your bathroom?"

That's right. I have my own bathroom now. It's attached to my bedroom and everything.

"Um," I say, not sure how to respond. Mom has never simply wanted to go shopping for something we don't desperately need. "When do you go to work?"

Mom's eyes flit to Landon's and he smiles, all straight teeth and dimples in his cheeks. "Honey, I'm not going back at all. I quit yesterday."

My eyes widen. "What? Why?"

She holds up her hands as if to signal to our elaborate surroundings. "I don't need to work anymore."

"I am happy to support all of us," Landon says, giving me a meaningful look. "I want Rose to be able to take some time off, focus on being a mom. She was working entirely too hard, don't you agree?"

I nod. She has been working a lot. And with a date night once every two weeks or so, Mom's schedule has been so full she's barely had time for us. I guess Landon wants to pay us back for that.

"That's really great, Mom." I smile so she knows I mean

it, and then I get back to her question. "But I don't really need anything. I have enough clothes."

"Nonsense. You live in Shady Heights now, and you're a part of our new family with Landon." Mom glances at him and he grins. They're both so gooey and in love and I'm not sure if it's cute or cringe-inducing. Maybe a little of both.

"While you ladies are shopping, I was thinking Pam and I could take the girls swimming." Landon turns to my little sisters. "What do you say? Want to go swimming?"

Emma squeals her excitement, and Starla, too young to know what swimming is, squeals just to be like her big sister.

"But they don't know how to swim," I say, turning to Mom. Surely she won't let her youngest daughters in harm's way?

"No worries. Landon used to teach swimming lessons in college, so he's really good," Mom says as if she can read my mind. "And we bought floaties and life vests for the girls, so they'll be totally safe." She leans in and touches my arm. "Plus, I was thinking when we get back from shopping, we could take a little dip ourselves. I haven't been in a pool in forever."

A swim *would* be nice.

But all of this is so overwhelming, I'm still waiting to wake up from the most realistic dream ever.

"I guess we can go shopping," I say, setting my fork down. "I mean, if you really want to."

"I insist," Mom says, putting a hand to her heart. "We're Shady Heights gals now. We need to look like it!"

Shady Heights gals?

I swallow the lump in my throat and push my chair back.

"Okay. That sounds fun, but I think I need to take a walk, if that's okay?"

"Sure," Mom says.

"Anything wrong?" Landon asks, his eyebrows drawn together.

I shake my head. "I'd just like a walk. Maybe get some fresh air."

The truth is, all of these changes are sucking the air out of my lungs. I feel like I'm on the verge of a massive panic attack, and yet my mother is smiling and laughing and acting like life is wonderful. I guess life *is* wonderful now.

But I could still use some fresh air.

8

———

COLBY

IT'S WELL past noon when I finally wake up on Saturday. Normally my parents will rag on me for "wasting my life" by sleeping in too late, but it's Spring Break so I get a little leeway.

I'm kind of expecting my parents to bitch at me for using the last of the bacon on my midnight snack last night, but when I venture down to the kitchen, I find them eating sandwiches and pouring over paperwork, a stack of bills next to them, and the checkbook opened. Looks like today will also be filled with stressing over finances.

I make a mental note never to live beyond my means, and try to heat up a frozen burrito without them noticing. Of course it doesn't work, and soon Dad is bitching at me for something I can't even control.

"You know how much your car insurance is?" he says, shaking his head.

"I haven't had any tickets," I say, watching the seconds

tick by on the microwave. Unlike my jackass friends, my driving record is spotless so far.

"It's not your record that's the problem," Dad says. "It's that fancy sports car."

The BMW was a gift from my parents on my sixteenth birthday. I didn't ask for it, and although I did want a car, I never asked them to get me anything luxurious. But they insisted, because it makes them look good. All of their friends buy luxury cars for their kids, so they did, too. And now I'm getting bitched at for it.

"Maybe I should just find a part-time job," I say, once again bringing up the topic they can't stand.

Mom snorts, looking up from her paperwork for the first time since I came in here. "No, honey. School is your first priority."

"But if I work, I can pay for my own car insurance and it'll take some of the stress off you guys."

Mom holds up her hand, her eyes as serious as her salon-styled hair. "No. I don't want to hear any more of that nonsense coming from your mouth."

I sigh. "Yes, ma'am."

Dad flips through some more bills and then looks up, as if seeing me for the first time. "Are you still here? It's Spring Break, right?" He shoos me with his hand. "Go outside or something."

Taking my burrito and a soda from the fridge, I leave them to their financial mess. Sometimes it feels like I should be the adult here, not my parents.

My phone has been blowing up all morning with texts from Bryce and Josh. They still want to hit up The Getaway, or go see a movie. Everything they want to do involves money, and I can't tell them I'm broke. Mom would no doubt have my head on a stake if I so much as hinted that the Jensen family wasn't loaded with cash.

Of course, there is a quick way to get some money and my parents can't complain about it. Mrs. Ruiz is an older woman who lives down the street, and she pays me to mow her lawn every few weeks. It's been a while since I've been over there, so I decide to see if she'd like to hire me today.

Changing into my worn out, grass-stained Nikes and a pair of basketball shorts, I head outside and walk the few blocks to her house. I don't wear a shirt in an effort to get a start on my summer tan, plus even though it's only March, it's already hot as balls out here.

Mrs. Ruiz is delighted to see me and asks if I can also help her water the many plants along her front and back porches. She usually waters them herself but her arthritis has been acting up. She says she'll pay me more money to do this, and I refuse, saying the thirty bucks for the lawn is all I need. I already feel kind of quilting for showing up just because I need cash.

I don't mind yard work. Mrs. Ruiz has a self-propelled mower so it doesn't even hurt my knees to push it through the grass, and her yard isn't as big as ours. With thirty bucks in my pocket, I can breathe a little easier knowing I'm good for at least two trips out with the guys if I budget my money right.

Mrs. Ruiz's Chihuahua starts barking like crazy from the front window where he likes to sit on the windowsill. I look over my shoulder as I mow, and see a girl about my age walking by. She's wearing leggings, a faded baggy T-shirt, and no shoes. She doesn't really look lost, not exactly, but there's something odd in her eyes.

I let the mower cut off, filling the air with silence. "Hi," I call out, trying to sound friendly. "Are you lost?"

She jumps, then turns in my direction. She has a pretty heart-shaped face and brown, shoulder-length hair. She certainly seems like she could be about my age, but I haven't seen her at school.

"No," she says, looking at me as if she's just been woken from a dream. "I'm fine."

"Okay," I call back, giving her a friendly wave. I crank up the lawn mower again, and get back to work. There's something in the way she walks, like either she doesn't have a care in the world, or like she has too many things on her mind. Part of me wishes I knew what it is, that I could ask her and see what's going on in her mind. But she keeps walking and I keep mowing, not taking my eyes off her until I have to turn the corner.

The end of Mrs. Ruiz's street is a cul-de-sac, so with any luck the girl will walk back my way before disappearing again. Sure enough, by the time I've finished mowing the front lawn, she appears again, this time walking up the other side of the road.

When the lawn is mowed and edged, I return the tools to the garage and get a water pitcher to help Mrs. Ruiz water her plants.

"You get these high ones," she tells me, pointing to the planters hanging from the porch roof. "I'll get the roses by the mailbox."

While watering the plants, I watch the girl approach. She's pretty, and I hate that I wish I knew who she was. For as jaded as I've been about girls and relationships lately, I should really stay away from them. But there's something in the cute way she walks with no shoes on that makes me want to get to know her. I can't picture the girls at school being so casual like that. They all need tons of makeup and coordinated outfits before they're seen in public.

I turn my attention to the last potted plant, a fern with red leaves, and then I hear Mrs. Ruiz cry out.

Dropping the water pitcher, I rush off the porch in time to see the girl reach out and catch Mrs. Ruiz right before she would have taken a painful fall to the concrete below.

I jog over. "What happened?"

"Goodness," Mrs. Ruiz says, her hands shaking as her dropped water pitcher spills water at our feet. She turns to the mysterious barefoot girl. "This girl is an angel," she says, her wrinkly cheeks lifting into a smile. "She saved me from falling. These house shoes are no good, I tell you. They make them so cheap these days."

"She scraped her hand on the mailbox," the girl tells me. "But I think she'll be okay."

"Let's get you inside," I say, taking Mrs. Ruiz's arm. "I'll get you some water."

"Oh, that's all right, sweetie." She brushes me off, preferring to stand unassisted. "I'll be fine. I'm not as tough as I used to be, but I'm okay."

She turns to our strange new visitor and takes her hand. "Honey, you should come in and have some sweet tea," she says. "It's the least I can do to thank you for saving me."

The girl's eyes widen, and I can tell she's surprised by the invitation. "Oh come on," Mrs. Ruiz says. "Let's all go have some sweet tea. What do you say?"

Even though I shouldn't care, even though I'm sick of dating, I bite the inside of my lip and pray that she says yes.

9

MADDIE

MY HEART RACES from what probably looked like a superhero dive when I stopped this elderly lady from falling. It's weird because I pretty much saw the whole thing in slow motion. I've been walking for half an hour, mostly just wandering up and down streets outside of Shady Heights while I try to get my bearings after this whirlwind of a weekend. Then a hot guy with no shirt on talked to me and tripped me up. I didn't want to walk back past him, but this stupid road has a dead end and I had no choice.

And then I saw her, her house shoes slipping off her toes as she stood on the curb, watering roses around her mailbox.

I was thinking to myself that this lady might fall if she leans any further over, and sure enough, she did. I managed to catch her before she hit the ground, and I can't even imagine what would have happened to her frail body if she fell on the concrete. I shudder at the thought.

But now my good deed has landed me directly in front of

the previously mentioned hot guy. Hot, *shirtless* guy. Did I mention he is shirtless? I can't seem to look away, even though I desperately should.

"You like sweet tea, don't you?" the woman says, patting my arm. She looks up at me with eager eyes, the kind of look you see on loving grandmothers, not that I've ever had one of my own. Both of my grandparents died many years ago. Something hurts my heart when I think about how kind this lady is, and I want to say yes. Of course I want to say yes because she's a nice old lady and I love sweet tea. I wouldn't even hesitate if it was just her and me.

But this guy is here, his longish hair all messy from the wind, his muscular arms glistening with sweat from doing the yard work and he's watching me with this curious smile that makes my knees weak.

"I'd love some tea," I hear myself saying, the logical part of my brain taking over for my heart. If it were truly up to me, I'd turn and run away because being this close to such a hot guy makes me nervous.

"Wonderful!" the lady says. "I'm Gloria Ruiz."

"Maddie," I say, looping my arm into her elbow as she offers it to me. "I'm Maddie Sinclair."

"Lovely name," she says, as we walk up the sidewalk toward her house. The guy follows behind us, and when I glance back at him, he gives me a smirky grin.

It almost seems like I've seen him before. Sure, he's super hot, but there's something familiar about him. I'm still wondering why he's familiar to me when we get on the porch and Mrs. Ruiz tells us she'll bring the tea and that we should relax and cool off from the heat.

"Maddie, hmm?" he says, pulling out a patio chair and sitting next to me, but at an angle so our knees are this close to touching.

"It's not short for anything," I say on habit. I get asked that a lot.

"Really?" He lifts an eyebrow. "Your real name is *Maddie?*"

I nod. "My mother isn't a fan of shortening names. She said why name me Maddison if I'd only ever be called Maddie?"

He chuckles. "I'm Colby, by the way."

And that's when it hits me.

This is Colby Jensen.

Star football player at Sweets High school, the pride of the Hornets football team up until a few months ago when he had to get surgery. I may be as far from the popular crowd as you can get, but even I hear that type of school gossip.

This guy is probably the most popular senior in our school. High school royalty always terrifies me. He's so popular, he's friends with the girls I saw in the ice cream shop, the stuck up bitches who know they're better than everyone else.

Breathing is suddenly hard, and I'm really wishing I would have run away when I had the chance. Any second now he'll realize I'm just a loser, poor trailer trash who Jacoby made sure to talk about to anyone who would listen. I don't exactly care what the popular crowd thinks of me, but I'd rather not see their sneer of disgust while I'm on Spring Break.

Mrs. Ruiz brings a pitcher of tea and three glasses with ice filled to the top. I breathe a little easier, grateful to have her here as a distraction. Now all I have to do is down this tea as quickly as possible and get the hell out of here.

"I haven't seen you around," Mrs. Ruiz says, taking a sip of her tea. She was right—her tea is pretty good. "Did you just move here?"

"Yes, kind of," I say, staring at the ice cubes in my glass. "We just moved in a few streets over and I thought I'd take a walk just to get some fresh air."

I know I'm no longer in Shady Heights, because that neighborhood is just a big circle filled with huge houses that all have gates or gatekeepers. I ventured into the next subdivision over, and although these houses are beautiful and probably still cost a fortune, they aren't the mansions in my new neighborhood. In fact, I'd feel a lot better if Landon lived in a house like Mrs. Ruiz. At least it's normal sized.

"Are you a senior?" Colby asks, leaning forward a little. He's so hot it's almost painful to look at him.

I nod.

"Awesome, I'll be happy to show you around school."

"That sounds like a great idea," Mrs. Ruiz says. "Colby is a great kid. He comes over and helps me around the house all the time. My own son won't even do it," she says, shaking her head.

"Well in my defense, she pays me," Colby says with a laugh.

Mrs. Ruiz chuckles and waves a hand at him. "It's well deserved."

Colby turns his attention back toward me. "So, where did you live before?"

I'm definitely not giving him the honest answer, so I decide on a more nuanced version of the truth. "We moved from this awful place," I say, waving my hand like it's no big deal. "It definitely seems better here."

He nods. "You'll like Sweets High. We're pretty chill and the teachers are okay."

Wait. Does he think I'm *new*, new?

I guess it makes sense that Colby Jensen wouldn't recognize me, the poor loser girl who only moved here four months ago. I mean, why would he? Popular guys don't see the rest of us.

I should probably tell him the truth, but again my brain just says something before I've thought it over. "Yeah, it seems okay. I mean school is school so it's never that great."

They both seem to agree with this statement. We sip on our tea and chat for a little while longer. I don't have to lie very much, but I definitely make no point in telling him the truth. School will be back in session in a few days, and I'll go back to being the loser who slips under the radar. I wouldn't doubt if Colby never talks to me again after today.

"Well, I should get going," I say, finishing off the rest of my tea. "My mother will wonder where I am since I didn't bring my phone with me." Right after I'd decided on taking a walk, Landon and Mom started talking about getting all of us new cell phones. I'm not sure why I'd need a new phone, because I hardly ever use mine as it is.

"Of course," Mrs. Ruiz says. "It was nice meeting you, Maddie. You come back now any time you want, okay?"

"I just might do that," I say. "Your tea was really good."

I tell her goodbye, and then give a weird wave to Colby. He gives me this wide grin, showing a set of perfect white teeth. Colby Jensen has longish dirty blonde hair that he leaves messy, like he's just returned from a day of surfing. There's a tiny scar on his left eyebrow, and that eyebrow quirks as he looks at me.

"I could walk you home if you'd like?" he says, rising from his chair.

I wonder if he'd still ask that if he knew I was the girl who lived in the pedophile house. "No thanks, I'll be fine."

"Well, I'm going home anyway, so I'll walk until we have to part ways."

Looks like I'm stuck with him. Luckily, Colby lives only three houses down from Mrs. Ruiz, so it's a short walk.

He stops at the end of his driveway, turning toward me. "Hey, so, I was thinking we could exchange phone numbers."

I lift an eyebrow. "Why would we need to do that?"

He gnaws on his bottom lip. "Well, I said I'd show you around school . . ."

Oh my God, is Colby Jensen *nervous*? This is the third time he's slipped his hand through his hair in the last few seconds. No way is this happening.

In my dreams I might get swept up in how hot he is and give him my number and pretend it would all be okay. But in reality, I am Maddie Sinclair, a senior who is about fifty thousand levels below him on the social popularity ladder. He doesn't mean what he's asking because he doesn't really know who I am.

"Maybe I'll see you around," I say instead, turning to

walk away with as much confidence as I can muster. Next time he sees me in the hallway at school, he probably won't even notice me.

"Damn," he says, grinning. "Guess I'll have to try harder next time."

10

———

COLBY

I HAVE TO GET A JOB. Even if my parents decide to disown me for it. I'm eighteen, and legally an adult, so if I want a job I should be able to get one. It's ironic, really. Most of the time teenagers are ridiculed for being lazy and a drain on their parent's finances, yet here I am desperate to help pay my own way and I'm constantly being told not to.

I want to go to college. I want to get a job I enjoy and then provide for myself in the way I want to. If they're not going to let me, then maybe I won't bother telling them.

By the time I get dressed and eat some lunch on Sunday, my parents aren't even home. They're out shopping for things we don't need, or dining somewhere that's too expensive.

I dress in a pair of khakis and a dark blue polo shirt, put on my best shoes and attempt to do something with my hair. I should probably get a haircut first, but I hate the idea of looking like every other guy in school. In my group of friends, my shaggy annoying hair is about the only thing that's mine.

When I look as trustworthy as businesslike as I can get, I head out in search of a job.

I know beggars can't be choosers, but I'd really rather avoid a job in food service. I don't want to be responsible for making people's food, or coming home smelling like grease, especially if I might actually keep this a secret from my parents.

After asking around at a few stores and being told they're not hiring, I pull into Marty's Fine Furniture, a big store inside a warehouse. They have annoying flashy commercials advertising their furniture as being the best quality around. Just thinking about it puts their jingle in my mind and I have to think of other songs so it doesn't get stuck there.

I head inside and find a manager on the store floor. His nametag says his name is Eric, and he tells me they're hiring furniture assemblers. When I cock an eyebrow, he explains that all of their supposedly "fine furniture" is shipped to them in boxes, and that the only thing that really separates them from other furniture stores is that they assemble it for you before you buy it.

It sounds easy enough, and the job pays well, plus he said the hours are flexible if I'm in school.

I ask for an application and only feel a little bit guilty about going behind my parent's backs. Eric has to help a customer, so he tells me to take my time filling out the application and just get back with them whenever I'm done.

I sit on one of the kitchen tables on display and begin filling out the form. This place is huge, and there are different departments for different rooms in each house. The kitchen section has about five billion different tables to choose from,

from nice looking stuff to weirdo furniture that I can't picture anyone ever buying.

I'm almost finished with my application when I hear a voice that sounds familiar.

"Where are you? This place is a maze," a girl says. It's Maddie, the same girl from yesterday, the one who'd left me hanging after I tried to get her number. Being rejected by a gorgeous girl was definitely a first for me, and that only makes me want to know her more.

I look up and find her standing just a few feet away, her back to me, while she talks on the phone. "I have no idea how this stupid phone works," she says, looking at the screen of her Samsung Galaxy and then putting it back to her ear. "Why is everything so complicated?"

She sounds frustrated, maybe even pissed off. But I can't just pretend I haven't seen her. She's way too pretty for me to ignore. Today she's wearing a pink dress that goes down to her ankles. She has a slight sunburn on her bare shoulders, like she went swimming yesterday.

"Okay, lime green couch. I'll look for it and you better be there," she says, before looking at the phone for a few seconds and then shoving it into her purse.

I flip my application over in case anyone wants to walk by and get a peek at my social security number, and then hop off the barstool and stride over to her.

"Good afternoon, ma'am," I say in a dorky accent that immediately makes me feel like a jackass. Pretty girls kind of do that to me.

Her eyes widen and then she flinches when she recognizes me. "Hey," she says, gazing down at my clothes. "You work here?"

"I'm applying for a job, but they haven't hired me yet."

"Well, good luck," she says, looking out at the vast warehouse of furniture and customers all around us. "I need someone to tell me where the lime green couch is."

"Looking for someone?"

She nods, squinting her eyes as she searches for the couch. "My mom. This place is so big I lost her." She pats the purse around her shoulder. "And this new phone is so stupid it took me forever to figure out how to call her."

"You seem like you're having a bad day," I observe. I get the urge to pat her shoulder and tell her it'll be okay, but if she wouldn't give me her number, she probably *definitely* won't be okay letting me touch her.

"Just too many changes," she says, almost absentmindedly.

I reach back and grab my application. "Come on, I'll help you look for the couch."

"Totally not necessary," she says, holding up a hand.

I take her hand and push it back down to her side. Her skin is soft and she smells like coconuts and sunshine, and I definitely don't want to let her go, but I'm also not some creep.

"Helping out a customer will look really good on my application," I say, holding up the paper. She grins and it makes my insides hurt because she's so freaking cute. Not at all like the girls I'm used to at school. Her smile is all innocent and sweet, not sultry and filled with hidden gold-digging motives. "Let's go find it," I say again, and this time she doesn't object.

Maddie walks slowly, taking in her surroundings as she goes, one hand wrapped around the purse strap over her shoulder. I'm such an idiot, I'm going over a million ways to maybe ask her to hang out sometime after this. She already turned me down for her number, but I don't want to give up.

There's something sweet about her, the way she smiles at little kids as we walk by, and the way she lets other people walk in front of her as we're weaving in and out of traffic. Most girls don't have that kind of common courtesy—at least not the girls I know. They're all about themselves, and expect everyone to bow down in front of them.

"So, are you looking forward to starting school?" I ask, just for something to say.

"Not really," she says with a snort. "I mean, who would be?"

"Touché." I rub my eyebrow. "Here's the living room area," I say, pointing out the obvious like the idiot that I am. "Now all we need is a lime green couch . . ."

"There she is," Maddie says, heading toward a woman who looks a lot like her, only older. She's sitting on the lime green couch and that thing is even uglier than I'd imagined. I mean, who buys a lime green couch?

When her mom sees us, her face lights up and she stands up and rushes over to us. "Maddie, I found the *cutest* bookshelf. I think you'll love it."

"I don't really need a bookshelf, Mom," Maddie says, lifting an eyebrow. She turns to me. "This is uh, Colby, right?"

My heartbeat quickens because she remembered my name and I nod like an excited puppy. *God, Colby, get it together.* "Yeah, I go to Maddie's new school."

Maddie clears her throat. "So, I'll see you around," she says, clearly trying to dismiss me.

"Oh, don't make him leave," her mom says, flashing me a grin. "Let him come help us shop."

Her mom turns to me and holds out her hand to shake mine. "I'm Rose," she says, giving me a sweet smile. I notice the massive diamond ring on her finger, and my heart drops into my stomach. That ring has to be expensive. Which means . . .

"Now let's go find some things! Money is no object," she says, waving as us to follow her as she spins on her heel back toward the area with bookshelves. "We deserve the best of the best."

There it is. An ache rises in my chest as I blindly follow along, even though I really don't want to anymore. Maddie sure seemed like a nice girl, but I was wrong about her. She's one of the wealthy, the elite, just like Maria. She'll probably start school and then be best friends with the M's in no time.

Sure, my parents put up a good front, but we're broke. I can't take her on the fancy dates she'll be expecting, and I can't buy her designer purses anytime she wants. No matter how much I might like her, I know there's no point in even trying.

There's no way she'll want to date a guy like me.

11

MADDIE

THERE'S a weird shift in Colby's demeanor after a few minutes of furniture shopping with Mom. Mom's not being rude or anything, so I don't know what's making him act so weird. He's been overwhelmingly nice ever since I met him yesterday, so I can't understand why he's suddenly staring at the floor, looking like he'd rather be anywhere but next to me.

My chest tightens. Maybe he finally figured out who I am, and he knows I'm not actually new to the school, just new to the neighborhood. But that can't be it because there's no way he knows me. Colby Jensen has never even been within fifty feet of me at school. We don't have any classes together, and I don't think Jacoby is close friends with him. So I'm just being paranoid.

Still, I think to myself as Mom starts fawning over a plush chaise lounge chair that we absolutely don't need, *did I really expect anything else?*

Colby isn't my friend. He won't like me when we return to school, so why am I actually excited that he wanted to walk with me in the store? It's better if I keep my distance. We aren't the type of people who could ever be friends, after all. He comes from money and popularity and I come from a dead broke single mom.

I feel like screaming because I'm so stupid, and I've so easily let an attractive guy pull down my protective walls. I take a deep breath and try to build them back up again, this time reinforcing them with invisible shields. No cute guy can break through them again, I'll make sure of that.

While Mom rattles on and on about how she definitely needs to buy one of those lounge chairs, I turn to Colby.

"You can go," I say, trying to sound casual. "Thanks for helping me find her, but this is boring and all. Plus, you have a job application to turn in."

He nods, his eyes not meeting mine. He seems to be lost in a dream world. "Yeah, okay." He gnaws on his bottom lip and then starts to walk the other way. "Nice seeing you again."

"He was cute," Mom says after Colby has safely walked out of earshot. At least my mom knows to be private about some things. She runs her fingers over a fringe tassel hanging off a couch. "Does he work here?"

"No, he goes to my school," I say, glancing back at his retreating form. He's halfway across the store now, reading over the application in his hand.

"You should date him," Mom says all matter-of-factly, like it's totally a normal thing to say.

I snort. "I don't even know him."

"You'll get to know him as you date him," she says,

pointing a finger in the air as if to punctuate her point. "That's the whole reason people date."

I shake my head. "He doesn't like me."

Mom's lips turn downward. "Well then he's an idiot and you can do better."

One time I saw this TV game show that took place in a store kind of like Wal-Mart. It was big and had tons of different items from clothing to electronics, and the game show contestants had to answer a series of trivia questions. Each question was worth a few seconds of time, and by the end of the round, all their awarded time got added up and they could take a shopping cart around the store, filling it with whatever they wanted until their time was up.

I used to daydream about being on that show, even though I was just a kid and didn't really know many answers to the trivia questions. My sisters weren't born then, so I would fantasize about getting lots of toys for myself, my own TV, new clothes. After a while, I *just* daydreamed about getting new clothes, probably because Brian Richard started making fun of me for only having three outfits to wear to school each day.

Shopping with Mom today makes me think of that game show. Mom snags a salesperson from helping another customer and starts rattling off items she wants to buy for our new house. It's technically Landon's house, but she calls it our house and says we should consider it ours as well.

"We are going to be a family soon," Mom says, gazing at

her massive engagement ring. "And not just a courthouse wedding family, but a real family. I'm going to have a real pastor marry us, right in the backyard."

"When is that happening?" I ask as we look at bookshelves, even though I don't need one. I don't even own any books.

"Soon," Mom assures me. "I was hoping you'd be my Maid of Honor, of course, and also I'd love it if you help me plan the wedding. We just want something small, just family only."

"I'd love to help you," I say. Oddly, I find that I really mean it. Our new life is a lot better than our old one, and Mom really loves Landon. I want this to work out for them. It'll be a much better home life for my sisters than I had growing up.

When we're finally done shopping, we follow the salesperson up to the front desk where he tallies up all of Mom's impulse buys. Since it's all furniture, we arrange for it to be delivered next week and that means we get to walk out of the store empty-handed, which is weird for how much money she just spent.

It didn't escape my notice that my mother, who has no credit cards anymore because her credit sucks, is now sporting a shiny new platinum Visa card with her name on it.

"Landon gave it to me," she says with a wink when she catches me eyeing it.

"So," Mom says, clapping a hand on my back as we step out into the parking lot. She slides her sunglasses on her head and turns to me. "This is the start of our new life, so I think we really need to celebrate it big."

"Isn't that what we just did?" I say, hooking my thumb over my shoulder to point at the furniture store.

Mom rolls her eyes. "No, silly. I'm talking about you and me. You're my oldest, and you've been with me through all the hell we've been through. Emma and Starla really have no idea, do they?"

My chest aches with the memories of my crappy childhood. Mom tried her hardest, but we never made it a whole week without worrying about money, bills, or food. "I'm glad their life will be better," I say, letting my head lean against Mom's shoulder for a second. "I'm really happy you met Landon."

"Me too, honey. And he truly loves me. He didn't even tell me about his wealth until we'd been dating a while, so he knew I wasn't just some gold-digger." Mom's eyes get big and she gazes off in the distance. "I fell in love with him for who he is, and he did the same to me."

"I'm really happy for you, Mom."

She grins and reaches for the keys to her new car. "I want to do something fun and drastic. I know! Let's get our nails done. Hair, too."

I hate myself for getting excited at the idea of something we could never afford to do a few days ago. But . . . "That sounds fun," I say, unable to hide my grin.

At a nearby salon, Mom and I sit in these fancy massage chairs with tubs of hot water at the bottom. Professionally skilled nail techs scrub the callouses off our feet and trim our toenails and paint them and everything. It is amazing.

I knew people got pedicures, but I just figured that meant

getting their nails painted. I had no idea how much went into it. It's so relaxing I could die.

Mom doesn't stop grinning in my direction, and when both our feet and hands look like a movie star's, she turns to me, giving me a coy look.

"I think we should do something drastic to our hair."

"Like what?" I say. My hair is brown, a little longer than my shoulders, and very very plain. I've never had a real haircut before—at least not one in a salon. Mom has a pair of hair shears and she's the one who gives us basic hair trimming when we need it.

We pay for our manicures and pedicures and then head over to the hair salon next door. "Hmm," she says, gazing at the photos of hair models all over the wall. "I'm thinking I should get some highlights, and maybe a nice trim to get rid of my split ends."

"Okay, I'll do that too," I say, suddenly eager to sit in one of the chairs and have someone else with actual talent do my hair for a change. As much as I'm trying not to be materialistic, I'm really having fun.

But maybe that's okay. This is our "new life" as Mom keeps saying. Maybe I'm allowed to have fun.

Our stylist's name is Bae, and she's tall and beautiful and has an amazing Jamaican accent. She loves mom's highlight idea, but when it's my turn to explain the style I want, Mom says, "Are you sure you want the same as me?"

"You don't have to choose right away," Bae says thoughtfully while she plays with my hair in front of a mirror. "We can do your mom's first, then you can decide."

"I don't really know what else to do," I say, shrugging. "I mean, anything will be better than my boring hair now."

"What do you suggest?" Mom asks Bae. "We're celebrating starting our lives over new and fresh, so I think Maddie should do something big and bold."

Bae purses her lips while she thinks it over. "Do you go to RCHS?"

I nod and her eyes light up. "They don't have a hair dress code in that school, so you could do a wild color if you'd like."

Mom's lips form an o. "Ooooh, you should, Maddie! I think that would look so cool! Maybe a rainbow of colors?"

Bae nods. "I could do that."

I bite my lip. Drastic hair colors? I've never even considered it. But we *are* starting over, and this *is* a new life, no matter how much I might still think of myself as poor trailer trash.

Plus, Colby thought I was a new girl.

What if I really become a new girl?

My lips twist into a smile and I turn to Bae. "Yes, let's do it. Only I'm thinking pink. Can you do pink?"

Bae nods, twisting a strand of my boring brown hair around her thin finger. "Totally, honey. I can do as pink as you want."

12

COLBY

JOSH HOVERS OVER MY SHOULDER, casting a shadow from the bright sun overhead. "Come on, man," he says. "Do it."

We're sitting on these fancy lounge chairs that his mom and sister use to get a tan. There's even a hole in the back of it for your face to fit in when you're lying on your stomach.

"I don't know, man." I set my phone in my lap and gaze out at the clear pool water. His pool is way nicer than ours, but then again his parents are a lot richer. "This seems kind of gross."

"Dude, tons of hot girls at your fingertips isn't gross," Josh says, sitting on the chair next to mine. He lays back and rests his hands behind his head. "It's genius."

I glance back at my phone, which is on the download screen for a local dating app. All I have to do is press the download button and I'll be on my way to, what the app calls, *thousands of eligible singles near you!*

"I'm not sure any meaningful relationship is ever made through a phone app," I say with a grimace.

"Colby," Josh says all serious like. He sits up and turns sideways on the chair, lacing his fingers together, elbows on his knees. "You're still a teenager. Chances are, you aren't going to find a meaningful relationship right now." He wiggles his eyebrows. "So why not have a little fun?"

I lay back, letting my head fit into the head hole in this chair as I gaze up at the blue sky. "I don't know why I let you talk me into this crap," I mutter. And then I download the stupid app.

Josh shows me how to set it up, but it's pretty easy. I put in my first name only, my age, and zip code. Then he makes me upload a picture, which he takes of me right now, so I'm wearing blue board shorts and no shirt, which kind of makes me feel like a douche. Josh swears it's a good thing.

"So now we just wait?" I ask.

He shrugs. "Or you can start picking girls yourself." On his own phone, he goes to the app and starts scrolling through pictures of girls within a twenty-mile radius. If you like them —based on picture alone, which isn't very romantic if you ask me—you heart their profile and they'll be alerted.

Josh hearts just about everyone.

"I think I'll wait and see who likes me first," I say, setting my phone on the concrete below my chair. "I can't believe you talked me into this."

He laughs. "For someone who's brother was so damn prolific with girls, I don't know why you suck so much at getting one."

"I know why," I say, taking in a deep breath so I can let it out in a sigh. "I actually care about what kind of girl I date. Greg dated anyone with nice boobs."

"True," Josh says. "I used to be like you, man. I've broken out of that, though."

This is a topic we haven't talked about, but I kind of wish we would. Of course, guys don't often get all mushy and emotional with each other. We're supposed to talk about "hot chicks" and only that. But the truth is, I've always been envious of my best friend.

Josh has had three serious girlfriends in his life, all of them lasting over a year. For teenagers, that's kind of a big deal. He's always seemed like the luckiest guy out of all of us —a pretty girl who cares about him on his arm at all of our parties. But last year, his last girlfriend, Elise, broke up with him for a guy in college at Texas A & M. It broke his heart, and he's transformed himself into a player ever since. He's dated probably a dozen girls since school started in August, and he acts like it makes him happy, but I'm not so sure it does.

"So, are you done having real relationships?" I ask, pushing dangerously close to the edge of what's acceptable to ask your guy best friend.

"Not done, done. Just . . . taking a break, I guess." Josh scrolls through girls on his dating app, making little facial expressions of approval or disapproval for each one. It's kind of barbaric, really, making a snap judgment of if a human being is worthy of dating based on their looks alone.

And it's not even their looks really, but just one single photo. I never look the same in every photo. Some make me look like a total troll, and others make me kind of, well, proud of my abs, that's for sure.

My phone buzzes like crazy, and I reach down and grab it. "Six new likes," I say, going to the app.

"Nice," Josh says, nodding in approval. He still hasn't taken his eyes off his phone.

I look through the photos of the girls who have all liked me. Well, some of them are girls. Two of my likes are women in their fifties. They're both married and looking for something "with no strings attached". Uh, no thank you.

"Can I put an age limit on this thing?" I ask, feeling like a total douche for declining these women's offers. It's just the tap of a red x on the screen, but I still feel bad. I wonder if the app will tell them I wasn't interested?

"Yeah, you can limit your options, but why would you?" Josh says.

"I'm not interested in hooking up with a fifty-four-year-old who has a husband," I say.

He laughs. "True that. Who else likes you?"

"A girl named Dia. She has face tattoos and her profile says she's currently three months pregnant."

"Uhhhh, pass," Josh says. He's hovering over my shoulder now. "Who's next?"

The next girl is pretty, with long brown hair and a full figure. She seems normal from her profile, but she lives a hundred and thirty miles away. So much for searching within my zip code.

The last like on my list?

"Damn!" Josh says, slapping me on the back. "You snagged an M again. Nice."

It's Maria.

"No way in hell," I say, trying really hard not to throw my phone into the pool and be done with it. I press the x next to her ridiculously inappropriate profile photo and drop my phone on my lap.

"She's hot and she's totally into you," Josh says. "Could be fun for a while."

"Been there, done that, remember? It's not happening again."

"You're no fun," Josh says, shaking his head.

"Honestly man, I just want a real girlfriend. Like, the real thing." I feel stupid saying it out loud, but it's the truth.

"I know," Josh says quietly. "I do, too. But my mom says that kind of crap doesn't happen when we're young. You have to be like twenty-five before you can even attempt to settle down with the right girl. Apparently we're not mature enough, and all that crap."

"Bull." I shake my head, something like anger tearing at my heart. I want the real thing. I want it now. I want to be a loving boyfriend to a girl who loves me back. I'm not too young for that and I refuse to be told I can't find something real right here and right now.

My phone beeps with a new text message.

Maria: Colby Jensen seeking love through a dating app? Never thought I'd see the day.

Me: Why the hell are you on there? Surely you harass enough guys in person on a daily basis.

Maria: Only you, sweetheart. Xoxoxo

I roll my eyes so hard they almost fall out. Luckily, Josh is absorbed in liking photos of girls on his phone that he doesn't ask who I'm talking to. I'd hate to lie to him.

I type up another text and hope she gets the hint.

Me: Good luck finding Mr. Right

While Josh chats up girls on his app, I decide to dive into the pool and try to take my mind off how I'm so pathetically in love with the idea of being in love. Not for the first time, Maddie's adorable heart-shaped face appears in my mind.

I close my eyes and dive toward the bottom of the pool, trying to think of anything but her, that cute way she smiles when she thinks I'm not looking, and the intoxicating smell of her coconut shampoo.

She's one of the elite, I remind myself. She's not into me. I can't give her anything she'd want.

I kick the bottom of the pool and swim back to the surface. *Stop thinking of Maddie, stop thinking of Maddie, stop thinking of Maddie.*

Maybe if I keep saying it, I'll be able to actually do it.

13

MADDIE

THE LAST FOUR days have been a dream come true. A surreal, insane, wonderful dream. I've spent most of my time with my mom and sisters, out at the pool or watching movies in the theater. And yes, Landon has a theater. He says it came with the house and he's never really used it before we moved in.

It has twenty reclining leather theater chairs that rise up toward the back of the room so that everyone has a good view, a massive TV screen, dark walls and a real popcorn maker. Between that, his pool table, the swimming pool, and our gorgeous bedrooms, there's really no reason to ever leave the house.

And now I have my own shiny platinum Visa card with my name on it. Landon and Mom gave it to me last night, saying they want me to be able to buy things I need without worrying about money. Although I thanked Landon profusely, I don't want to use his money. It's just weird.

Of course, what's even weirder than being given a credit

card with no limit, is the question he just asked me at the breakfast table.

"Um, excuse me?" I say over a bite of pancakes. Surely I heard my future step-dad wrong. There is just no freaking way.

"Well . . . you're seventeen," Landon says, cutting into his pancakes with his fork. "The school buses don't run on this part of town, and you need a reliable mode of transportation. Rose and I had a blast buying her car, and so I'd love to take you to get your own car today."

Mom brightens, like she's been waiting all day for him to spring this offer on me. "I have an idea," she says, smiling so wide I can see nearly all of her teeth. "Why don't you and Landon go car shopping together and I'll stay here with the girls? That way you can get some bonding time in."

"I would be delighted," Landon says. He looks at me with this proud yet nervous smile, and I can tell he really wants to make a good impression on me. But he's already done enough to win my praise and my recommendation to Mom.

A car?

I really don't need a car.

"Thanks, but . . . I don't want to ask that much of you."

"It's not asking much," Landon says. "I've always wanted my own kids, but I never had any, and buying them a car has always been a dream of mine. I'm a car guy, after all."

I gnaw on my lip as I remember the tour he gave us the day we moved in. The garage is nearly as big as the house, and Landon has a truck, a Jeep, and three fixed up classic cars that are probably worth a ton of money.

"Well, I mean . . . if you really want to," I say, turning to look at Mom. My bright pink hair falls over my shoulder, still a surprise to see since I'm not used to it.

"I do want to," Landon says.

"You need a new car!" Emma says, shoving a huge mouthful of sausages mixed with pancakes and syrup in her mouth. "You need a blue car!"

"Red car!" Starla says, grinning her little toddler grin.

"Or a pink car," Mom says, throwing me a wink.

I swallow and set my fork down. The sheer idea of getting a brand new car just given to me is so exciting and scary that I'm not even hungry anymore. "Okay," I say, partly because cars are awesome and also because I don't feel I have much of a choice. "Let's go car shopping."

Landon stops for Starbucks on the way to the dealership. I feel kind of stupid because I have no idea what to order and the menu is so varied that I can't really decide. We've never had money for luxuries like five-dollar coffee before.

I ask Landon to choose for me, and he orders two Java chip frappuccinos. It is delicious, and I totally approve.

"So, how are you settling into your new life?" he asks when we pull out of the Starbucks drive through and head back onto the highway.

"It's definitely crazy, but I'm adjusting," I say with a little laugh. "I really am grateful for all you're doing for us."

"I'm happy to," he says. "I'm sorry it's all happened so fast. We didn't mean for that at all, and Rose and I both kind of kept things reserved at first. I didn't let her know how wealthy I was, and she—" He heaves a sigh, his hands gripping the steering wheel a little tighter. "She didn't tell me how bad things were for you guys. I knew she wasn't well off, and I knew she hated working at Savings Mart, but we planned to start introducing our relationship to you guys slowly. I wanted to take you and the girls out to dinner a few times, stuff like that. But then when Rose said something about the drug raid on the trailer next door keeping her up at night, it didn't sit right with me. I had to see for myself what kind of living situation you had and it just . . ."

He shakes his head, a frown forming on his lips. "It just killed me. I didn't know things were that bad, and now that I did know, well I had to get you out of that situation. Kids are precious and they should never have to live like that."

"That's really kind of you," I say. I've been told similar things from the men in Mom's past, but they've never felt this sincere.

"I love your mom, Maddie. I really do. And I wish we had moved slower so you could really get to know me before moving in, but still hope things work out well. I want us to be a family, and I want you to know you can come to me with anything, okay?"

Maybe it's just the caffeine and sugar rush, but I can't help but smile. "Thank you."

"So," he says, his demeanor getting more upbeat. "Do you know what type of car you want?"

I lift my shoulders. "I have no idea. A car, I guess. Not an SUV or anything."

He chuckles. "We can test drive them all if you want. I'd

suggest something with a sunroof because those are fun. And a good sound system, too."

I nod along, looking out the window at all the cars we drive by. I have never in my life been in a position to care about cars, much less daydream about getting a new one. Where would I even begin?

"What kind of car is that?" I ask as a gorgeous midnight blue sporty car zooms past us. It's low to the ground and looks sleek and kickass. There's a Chevy symbol on the back of it, but it goes by too quickly to see anything else.

"A Camaro," Landon says, nodding. "Excellent car. That was my first car ever, actually."

"Hmm," I say, watching it disappear ahead of us. "A Camaro. Can we look at those first?"

"Hell yeah," he says. "I might have to get a second one for myself."

Two hours later, I'm sliding into the front seat of my shiny new Chevy Camaro. It's silver, with black leather seats and a sunroof.

And it's all mine.

Landon even had them put the car's title in my name. I slide my hands over the steering wheel and breathe in deeply, reveling in the wonderful new car smell.

Landon finishes talking with the sales guy, who happens to be someone he knows in some business way or another, and then he walks over to me. He taps the top of the car, while I sit inside with the driver's side door open.

"I can't thank you enough," I say.

"As long as you're happy, I'm happy," he says. "I just

talked to Rose and she said they're having fun in the pool. You wanna stop and get some lunch before we head back?"

"Sure," I say, and I really mean it. None of Mom's other boyfriends have ever asked me to lunch, just the two of this. This guy is pretty awesome.

We go to a Mexican restaurant and the food is absolutely to die for. I'm starting to wonder if I've just eaten the wrong things all my life. Peanut butter sandwiches and cheap instant noodles are no way to enjoy meals, that's for sure.

"Do you need a parking pass at the high school?" Landon says over the smoking tray of his fajitas.

"I don't know. I think so, yeah."

"When I went to school there, they'd tow you away if you didn't have a pass, so we'll make sure we get one."

"Good to know," I say. Now I'm realizing I might not even know the fastest route from my new neighborhood to the school. I should probably figure it out before school starts back.

"Next Spring Break we'll go on vacation or something," Landon says. "This one is too boring staying at home all week."

I snort. "Trust me, it hasn't been boring."

He laughs. Conversation comes easy with him, and that's good. He's genuinely a nice guy and not some creep, and my secret worries that maybe he's a serial killer are slowly going away.

"Your friends at school won't even recognize you with the new hair and car, I bet."

I roll my eyes. "I don't really have friends, so I'm not too worried about it."

Colby flashes into my mind, no matter how hard I've been trying to ignore him. "Hey, Landon, I actually have a question for you, if you wouldn't mind."

"Go for it," he says, reaching for some tortilla chips.

"So I ran into some people from my school the other day when I was shopping," I say, turning the Colby story into a made-up version of the truth. "They thought I was a new girl and offered to show me around school. And, well, I just kind of froze up and didn't tell them I've been going there for four months. I just let them think I *was* new."

"That'd be a fun social experiment," he says, chewing thoughtfully. "Go back as the new girl and see how many friends you get with pink hair versus your normal hair."

"I don't think it's the hair," I say, glancing down at my manicured nails. "I think it's the whole she-bang. I live in Shady heights now, so I'm not seen as some parasite from the trailer park."

He grimaces at this, but then looks at me with sincerity in his eyes. "Are you asking me what you should do?"

"Kind of, I guess. If I see those same people at school again, they're gonna think I'm new and I don't know if I should just tell them the truth or not."

"Eh, it's only high school. I say live boldly. You can be a new girl if you want to be. After all, Rose is all about starting over fresh and leaving behind your old life. If that will make you happier in the end, I say go for it."

I grin. "I like the way you think."

Landon studies his food for a moment. "I grew up in a situation a little like yours. My dad was an alcoholic who beat the hell out of my mom."

I flinch at his candid confession, but I don't say anything and let him continue. "She died when I was seventeen. Cancer, but I know my dad's crappy treatment of her didn't really help. I moved out, got a scholarship to college, and never went back again. I did the same thing you're doing now, in a way. I started over. I became a new person with a new life and I didn't mourn the old one at all. Sometimes we just need that, you know? We deserve to be happy."

I nod, grateful that he's shared this part of his past with me. If I can take this opportunity and start over, then maybe I can be happy. Maybe I *do* deserve the happiness.

Maybe even I can deserve someone like Colby. Butterflies erupt in my stomach at the thought.

I wonder if it's too late to give him my number?

14

COLBY

MY PHONE RINGS early on Thursday morning. Way too early for a friend to be calling, and I almost sleep through it, but then I decide to check the caller ID.

It's Marty's Fine Furniture, and I sit up in bed, clearing my throat.

"Hello?" I say, putting the phone on speaker.

"Hi, is this Colby Jensen?"

"Yes, sir," I say.

"This is Julian from the hiring department at Marty's Fine Furniture, and I have your application here," the voice on the other line says. My heart skips a beat. "Unfortunately, we can't hire anymore for the next quarter, but we will be hiring again in June. Would you like me to save your application and give you a call back then?"

My heart falls, and I rub my hand slowly over my face, letting the disappointment sink in. "Yes, I'd still like to be considered this summer," I say, trying to be hopeful since three months isn't too far away.

We talk a little more and then he promises to call me back in a few months. When the call ends, I set my phone back on the nightstand and prepare to go back to sleep. It's only eight-thirty in the morning, after all, and I am not all about that.

My dad appears in the doorway of my room, his lips pressed into a thin line.

"What's up?" I say, suppressing a yawn.

"Marty's Fine Furniture?" he says, stepping inside my room. My blood turns cold. "What the hell have we told you about getting a job?"

It is too early and I am too tired to get in an argument right now. "I just wanted to help you guys out," I say.

"You are the *kid* and I am the parent," he spits. "You should trust that I can take care of this family. I just closed a great deal on a new client, by the way," he says, reaching into his pocket and taking out his wallet. "You just need to have a little patience," he hisses. He pulls out two hundred dollar bills from his wallet and tosses them on my nightstand. "Go have fun with your friends."

He lets my door close a little harder than necessary when he leaves, and I flop back on my bed with a groan. Parents are weird.

The next time I wake up, it's to the sound of multiple text messages blowing up my phone. At least now it's a little before noon, which is a perfectly acceptable time to wake up on Spring Break.

I take a piss and then check the messages.

Josh: Only 4 more days of sb. What we doin?

Josh: Getaway? Beach? I got gas $

Josh: dude, wake tf up

The beach does sound fun, but it's an hour drive away, which uses up a lot of gas. Josh's parents own the Flying Mermaid, a surf shop on the water. It's the perfect place to hang out when we do go to the beach, but I'm not really feeling it tonight. Spring Break on the beach sucks because a million other people are there, especially now that it's the last weekend before school starts back up.

I'm about to text him back, when I get a new group message.

Mindy: party at my house, 7pm. You bitches are invited.

Mindy has been one of my close friends since we were in the same play group as three-year-olds. She lives in Shady Heights, the nice neighborhood right next to mine, and she's also one of the M's. Of course, she's the nicest one, even if she's a bit . . . materialistic. Plus, I like her because we've never been into each other in a sexual way. She's my bud, and she's cool to hang out with.

Of course, if she's there, the other M's will be too, and that means I'll have to deal with Maria.

Josh sends me another text.

Josh: Or mindys party? What do ya say?

I consider my options, and then decide that I'm sick of making decisions. I'm also sick of going places specifically because I hope to meet a girl. This time, I'll let fate decide for me. Or, well, Josh.

Me: Your call.

Josh: Mindy's party will be lit. Lets go there

Me: k. be here at 7. We'll walk over

PAM WAKES me up on Saturday morning by lightly tapping on my door. I'm still not used to having a maid make my bed every day and clean up after me, even though I try really hard to keep things clean so she doesn't have to work as much.

"Is everything okay?" I ask, sitting up in bed.

"Ms. Rose asked me to get you," she says. "There's visitors here and she wants you to meet them."

I quirk an eyebrow. "Visitors?"

Pam nods and slips into my room, picking up the dirty clothes I'd tossed on the floor last night. I cringe inwardly, wishing I had remembered to put them in the hamper.

I get dressed quickly, in a pair of jean shorts and a T-shirt, then pull my hair back in a ponytail.

I hear friendly chatting down in the living room, and when I get down there, one of the most popular girls in the school is standing in the foyer, a beautiful older woman standing next to her.

"Here's my daughter," Mom says, ushering me over. I recognize the girl from school, though I don't know her name. She's one of the M's, though, the one with dark blue tips at the bottom of her dark hair. My cheeks flush red the second she looks at me, and I just know she's going to recognize me, call me out for being the fraud that I am.

"Oh my God, I love your hair!" she says instead.

"Um, thanks," I say, glancing from her to her mother. "I like yours, too." Landon is holding a massive gift basket filled with wines and cheeses.

"These are the Carmichaels," he says, shifting the gift basket to his other arm. "They came over to welcome you to the neighborhood. They live two houses down."

"I'm Mindy," the girl my age says. "Are you a senior?"

"Yes," I say dumbly, followed by, "I'm Maddie."

This makes her mom giggle, and Mindy's eyes go wide. "Oh my God, another M! How awesome is that?"

"Another M?" I ask, pretending like I don't already know that Mindy and her friends are called the M's.

Landon asks Mindy's mom something about the homeowner's association, and Mindy walks closer to me, lowering her voice so it's like we're the only two people here. It's weird how badly I want her to like me.

"The M's are my best friends. There's me, Maria, and Matilda. We've all known each other for, like, ever."

"That's really cool," I say, feeling like more of a moron with every stupid thing that comes out of my mouth. She loops her arm into mine and flashes me a brilliant popular girl smile.

"And now you can be our fourth M. I'm having a party at

my house tonight, so you should totally come over and meet everyone."

I nod, a feeling of excitement falling over me. This is the first time I've been invited to anything in my high school years. Little kid birthday parties don't really count in this type of situation.

"Sounds fun," I say, trying for casual, but probably totally failing.

"Great. It's a pool party, so wear your skimpiest bikini," she says, giving me a wink. "We'll have food, too, so don't eat beforehand."

"Awesome."

"I'm just two houses down," she says, staring at her cuticles. They're just as nicely manicured as mine are, and I realize that to a stranger, we'd look like we belong together in the same social clique. Maybe now we do.

"Which direction are you?" I ask, nodding toward the front door.

"That way," she says, pointing to our left. "It starts at seven but you can come early if you want. That way you can scope out which guy you'd like to flirt with before some other girl gets him."

Again, she winks, and then she releases my arm and I'm suddenly back in the real world, free of her captivating spell.

So that's what it's like to be in with the popular crowd.

I think I like it.

"I am so proud of you," Mom coos as soon as the Carmichaels have left. "You made a new friend! I knew this move would be good for us."

I roll my eyes. "Do you have a bathing suit? I need one for her party."

"No, but . . ." Mom's eyes flash with that grin that I've come to know so well this week. "Looks like we should go shopping."

I never thought I'd be sick of shopping, but I totally am. I've done enough of it this weekend to last a lifetime, but Mom's right. I need a bathing suit, especially if I'm going to be properly introduced to the M's today.

So we head to the mall and Mom shoves me into a fitting room with an armful of bikinis. They're all cute, but I feel naked when I step out and model them in front of the three sided mirror. Of course, that's probably because I am practically naked.

These things are skimpy, and probably exactly what Mindy had in mind. I don't think the M's have a problem wearing these in public, so I shouldn't either.

I settle on a hot pink suit with lace trim. It matches my hair, and the bottoms tie at the sides and it's really cute. Mom also encourages me to pick out some new flip flops, which I get, along with a beach towel and a mesh mini dress swimsuit cover-up.

By dinner time, I'm nervous as hell. I only nibble on the bacon cheeseburger our chef cooks up on the grill, even though it's greatest burger I've ever had.

I am keenly aware that Mindy's party will be filled with

popular students. No doubt, all of the RCHS "in" crowd will be there. And that means Colby might also show up.

This fact alone has me questioning my bikini choice as I stand in front of my bathroom mirror, looking at my body. It's not a terrible body, but it's also nothing special. I don't have much of a tan, and knees are all scarred up from when I learned how to ride the neighbor's bike when I was a kid.

But my nails are cute, and my hair is awesome, and Mindy seems to like me, so maybe her approval will make other people like me as well. Maybe I can really pull this off.

Maybe I'll get the guts to flirt with Colby. And maybe it'll all work out.

16

COLBY

THERE WAS a time when we lived in the best neighborhood in Louetta. My parents made sure to talk about it from the second they bought our house on that very first day when I was five years old. We were "moving on up" as the saying goes.

Then a few years later, they cleared the land to the east of our neighborhood and built Shady Heights, much to my parent's chagrin. They've been wanting to move to the bigger, more expensive neighborhood ever since.

Josh rambles on about how he's being talking to this girl from his dating app, but she lives thirty miles away so they haven't met yet. We're walking over to Mindy's house, which takes about ten minutes by foot, and that's exactly how long my idiot best friend talks about this girl.

I don't really listen to much of it. I uninstalled the app from my phone the same day I downloaded it. It's not worth my time to deal with girls on a stupid app. When I find something real, I want it to be *real*, not digital.

Bryce texts me saying he'll be late because he's stuck doing yard work for his parents. I'm a little relieved, because the guy can be a bit—loud—annoying—take your pick, at parties. At least we'll get a little time to chill before he arrives and embarrasses the hell out of me.

Mindy's housekeeper lets us inside her house, where the party is happening in the backyard. They have a massive pool house with one wall that's solid glass doors that slide open, making the entire pool house open to the outside. It's a pretty sweet set up, and I've been swimming here since I was little so I know it all as if it were my own house.

The party is already pretty packed by the time we arrive. Most of the football team is here, and they surround me the moment we step on the back patio. I'm given a beer, which I drink quickly, hoping to get more in the party mood.

When I'm on my second beer, I start eyeing the hot tub. That thing would make my knee feel so much better, since it's been aching lately.

I nudge Josh, who's deep in a text conversation with internet girl. "Let's go to the hot tub. No one's in there yet."

"Dude, I'm not getting in a hot tub with you unless girls are in it, too."

"Fine," I say, as our quarterback walks by, tapping his beer bottle to mine in a hello. "I'll go alone."

I make my way through the crowd of people, the hot tub sounding better and better with each step closer.

Someone calls out my name in a high-pitched, drunken girl voice, and I look over. The first thing I see is a shock of hot pink hair.

The second thing I see are the M's.

Maria narrows her gaze on me, a lion ready to devour her prey. Mindy is the girl who called my name, and she's waving me over now, but all I can focus on is the girl next to her.

The pink hair is new, but the smirky adorable face is not. That's Maddie, standing right here with the M's, as if she belongs.

Now that I think about it, I guess she does. Even her name fits in with them.

"How's it going?" I tell Mindy, raising my beer bottle in a quick hello.

"I'm introducing everyone to my new friend," Mindy says, putting an arm around Maddie and shoving her forward a step. "Colby this is Maddie. She's new, so I want you to be nice to her."

Maddie gives me a little wave. "Hey," she says, and it could be my imagination, but I'm pretty sure her cheeks are turning the same color as her hair.

"I like the hair," I say, grinning at her like the fool that I am. I turn to Mindy. "We've already met, actually. Just a couple days ago."

"Okay asshole," Mindy says, throwing me a playful glare. "You're supposed to alert me when you meet new girls that are totally perfect for my exclusive group of beautiful best friends."

"Sorry," I say, taking a sip of my beer. Maddie's eyes haven't left mine, and I give her a smirk. "Maybe I just wanted to keep her to myself."

Okay, I think two beers have already done me in. Normally, I wouldn't be so bold to flirt with a girl who has turned me down before. Of course, no girl has ever turned me down in the past, so maybe I don't really know what I'm capable of.

I'm vaguely aware of how Maria is slowly turning into a human flamethrower, her jealousy making her lips twitch, but it's not my fault that I like someone else. It's not like I've been leading her on or anything; it's actually quite the opposite. I've told her twice in the last few days that I'm not interested.

So she can get over it.

Mindy smacks her lip gloss. "Well, Maddie is my new friend, so I trust you'll take care of her, okay?"

"I'd love to take care of her," I say. As badly as my eyes want to trail down Maddie's body, taking in all of the curves her see-through dress barely covers, I keep my gaze focused on her face. "Unfortunately, you might need to find someone else, because I don't think your new friend likes me very much."

Maddie's cheeks flush even more and she opens her mouth like she's going to object, but Mindy beats her to it. "What did you do to her, you pig?" she says, putting her hands on her hips.

"Nothing," I say, holding up my hands in surrender. "I just asked for her number and she shot me down."

Matilda, who up until now had been playing on her phone, looks up and laughs. "Nice," she says, giving an approving look to Maddie. "Colby could use a girl who keeps his ego in check."

Mindy nods, throwing an arm around Maddie. "Hmm,

come here," she says, motioning me forward. She pushes Maddie toward me, then takes our arms and lines us up until we're standing next to each other. I can smell Maddie's coconut shampoo again, and it makes something flutter in my stomach.

Now Mindy steps back, thumb and finger on her chin while she surveys us. "Ya'll do make a cute couple . . ." She glances over at the other two M's for confirmation. Matilda wobbles her hand back and forth like she's torn on the answer, and Maria just glares at me.

If she could shoot daggers out of her eyes, I'd no doubt be dead by now.

"Okay, ya'll are cute together, but step aside Colby," Mindy says, shooing me away with her hand. "Before I hook you up with my new friend, I need to make sure there's no better options available."

I grin, knowing Mindy loves messing with me. Maddie still hasn't said much this whole time, but it almost seems like she might have changed her mind about me. Or maybe she's considering it. She's definitely not looking at me like she hates me.

I decide to play it cool, and let the cards unfold as they will.

"I see how it is," I say, taking another sip of my beer. "I'll be in the hot tub if you change your mind."

I wink at Maddie and it makes her bite her lip nervously, which makes me feel amazing.

As I'm walking away, I stop in front of Mindy and lean in, pretending to whisper but really keeping my voice loud enough for Maddie to hear.

"You know I'll take good care of your girl," I say.

Mindy rolls her eyes and shoves me away. "Get out of here. I'll decide if you're worthy when I feel like it."

17

MADDIE

I WATCH COLBY WALK AWAY, the muscles in his back tightening as he lowers himself into the hot tub. I'm not exactly sure how this popular crowd does things in regards to flirting, but that was fun.

Mindy keeps her arm around my shoulders, even as she talks to another guy who looks like he's had too many beers and too much sun this Spring Break. When he leaves, she turns to me.

"So, are you totally free from wherever it is you came from?"

"Huh?" I ask. Although I've turned down the beers that have been offered to me, I kind of wish I was drunk right now, that way all of my stupid questions would at least be justified.

"Free from guys," she says, giving me a sultry look. "There's not some long-term boyfriend back at home thinking you're waiting for him or anything?"

I laugh. "Nope. Definitely not."

"Excellent! Let's find you a man. As my girls can

confirm," she says, gesturing to the two other M's, "I am an excellent matchmaker."

"Excellent is purely her opinion," one of the M's says. It's the curvy Latina girl with the short hair, and I'm pretty sure her name is Maria. I accidentally forgot the other girl's name, but she's been so quiet that you can't really blame me.

"Oh hush," Mindy tells Maria. To me, she says, "You tell me what type of guy you want, and I'll make it happen."

Maria just scoffs, folds her hands over her chest and looks away. She's clearly pissed, but Mindy doesn't even register it.

"Well, if we're talking guys," I say, trying to be bold for once in my life. "Colby isn't too bad."

I glance over at him. He's looking right at me, steam rising from the hot tub. He makes a "come here" motion with his finger and it sends a chill down my spine.

"Eh . . ." Mindy says, waving at some girls as they walk by and say hello to her. "Colby is all right, I guess."

"Oh, wait." A knot twists up in my stomach as I realize what's probably going on here. "I'm sorry, I didn't realize. Did you two date?"

She shakes her head. "Nope, he's not my type."

I lift an eyebrow. "He's totally hot. What exactly is your type?"

She motions for me to follow her and we slowly walk around the large pool.

"I like older guys. Mid-twenties, thirty. Unfortunately, most of them won't even touch a seventeen-year-old, so I'm choosing to stay single until college, and then it's open season on some mature older guys."

She wiggles her eyebrows and it makes me laugh. "Hey, whatever makes you happy, I guess."

"I'm just so over high school guys," she says. "I want someone who lives on their own, without parents getting in the way and stuff. I want someone mature."

A guy holds out a shot glass and Mindy takes it, downing the liquor in just one gulp. I'm kind of surprised that no one cares that I'm not drinking. I guess years of watching TV has had me conditioned to think I'd be ridiculed for turning down alcohol.

But maybe being with the exclusive M's has certain privileges, like the right to do whatever you want.

"I think it'd be hot to date a single dad," Mindy says, blowing a kiss at someone from across the pool. "Your stepdad Landon is *so* freaking hot."

"Eww," I say, shoving her in the arm. She laughs. This conversation is definitely not going in the direction I'd prefer. I decide to bring it back around to the important topic.

"If you're serious about setting me up, I vote Colby," I say.

Her lips slide to the side of her mouth. "Let me tell you about Colby. Me and him are pretty close, actually. I've known him my whole life."

"So what's wrong with him?"

"Nothing. Not really. He's just . . . He's kind of obsessed with trying to be someone besides his brother. He's always compared to him, especially when it comes to girls. Greg had this reputation of being some kind of sex god, and I know Colby gets a lot of crap for it because he doesn't date as much as Greg did."

She tosses her long hair over her shoulder, the blue tips catching the light from the string of patio lights above. "If you *really* like him, I'd support it. But you're new and you're totally hot and you could get any guy. So I say you take your time."

"You're different than I thought you'd be."

Crap. The words are out of my mouth before I realize what I'd just said. Crap, crap, crap.

Mindy quirks an eyebrow. "What do you mean by that?"

What I meant was that I'd spent four months seeing her and her posse of M's prance around the school like the royalty that they are, and I figured they'd all be bitches with their own agendas. And yet here she is, being a real friend to me, not at all like what I'd expected. But I can't tell her that, or my cover will be blown.

I shrug and gaze off at the pool as if there's something super interesting going on in there. "Just . . . first impressions from this morning I guess."

"Yeah, sorry about the exuberant wine basket," she says, waving a hand. "My mom goes a little crazy welcoming people. But I swear to you, I'm a nice person."

Not to the losers in school, I think.

Mindy continues. "We're all nice, except maybe Maria, who I think is kinda pissed that I invited a new girl into our group, but she can get the hell over it. She's been so moody lately, it's annoying. I keep telling her to get the hell over herself but it doesn't really work." She rolls her eyes. "Anyhow—"

But I don't hear what she says next. These two huge guys get in a shoving fight and suddenly I'm knocked into so hard it takes the breath out of my lungs. I go flying, and I trip over my own feet. There's a splash and then another one, and I'm sinking into the cold water.

So much for my hair looking nice, I think as I flounder around, my feet touching the bottom of the pool. I push myself up and gasp for breath as soon as I resurface.

Someone whistles.

That's when I realize my top fell off.

I drop low, burying my top half under the water, but there's lights in the pool and it feels like everything is glowing too much. In the distance, I hear Mindy yell at one of the guys who started the shoving fight, calling him a clumsy oaf.

Some of the drunk guys whistle and catcall in my direction. I look around frantically for my bikini top, but there are too many people in the pool and too much commotion going on for me to find it.

Tears flood my eyes.

"Hey, new girl!" I look over to find a chubby guy with short brown hair holding up my pink bikini top with one finger. He gives me a creepy grin. "Show me them boobies again, and you'll get this back."

I am frozen. I can't find a single thing to say, and all I can do is wish I wasn't here. Anywhere but here.

I try to look for Mindy, but there's so many people, partying, dancing, drinking. I can't find her.

Someone appears next to me in the pool. I'm shoved behind him, my chest pressed against his back, his hand protectively holding me against him to shield me from prying eyes.

Wet, dirty blonde hair makes me realize it's Colby.

"Alright, idiot," he says. "Toss it over or I kick your ass."

"You're no fun, Jensen." The chubby guy tosses it and Colby catches it in the hand that's not holding onto me. Then he walks backward, until I'm caught between him and the large rocks of the built-in waterfall of the pool. It's about as private as we can get since there are so many people around. Colby hands me the bikini top over his shoulder.

"Thanks," I mumble, and I take it, dipping below the water to put it on. But it's a string bikini that knots around my back and neck, and unfortunately, Mom helped me tie the first knot around my back.

When it's fastened around my neck, I turn toward Colby.

"Um . . . could you maybe . . . help?"

He turns around to face me, his eyes closed. "Can I look?"

"Yeah," I say. I'm holding the triangle pieces over my boobs. "Could you tie it around my back, please?"

"Sure thing," he says. From this close, he's even cuter. My heart is pounding like crazy, and this time it's not because I just embarrassed the hell out of myself in public. I turn around and pull my hair over my shoulder.

Colby's fingers take the strings and tie them. He moves slowly, his skin like fire when it touches mine. He's so close, I could just lean back and be pressed against his chest. The urge to do that is overwhelming.

"Okay, I think you're good," he says.

If my life were a movie, maybe I would turn around and kiss him. Instead, I say, "Thanks."

He grins, his face hovering just inches from mine. "Anytime."

18

COLBY

IT'S NOT VERY OFTEN that I want to kick someone's ass, but Robbie Carter sends my anger through the roof. It is not okay to taunt a girl with her own bathing suit top. And every other prick who laughs along with him is now on my shit list.

"Don't worry about that jackass," I say once Maddie's bathing suit is now back in place.

I can still feel the way her bare chest fit against my back, and I try really hard to shove those thoughts to the back of my mind. It's not every day you feel a girl's boobs before you've even taken her on a date.

"Thanks for helping me," Maddie says. Her pink hair is a lot darker when it's wet, and she's somehow even cuter with mascara running down her cheeks.

Our eyes meet, and it makes my stomach seize up. She is so beautiful, and the words are on the top of my tongue. I probably shouldn't say it, shouldn't admit how weak she makes me.

Maybe I should talk to Mindy about her, get a feel for if I

could ever have a chance with someone like Maddie. I know she's well off, and now she moved here and slipped seamlessly into the most popular group of girls in school.

Even as a former football star, that makes her out of my league.

But I still want to try.

"You okay?" she asks, reaching a hand out of the water and touching my cheek. My skin warms beneath her touch and I can't help but grin.

"I'm perfect," I say. Her lips curve up, and for a little while it's almost like we're the only two people on earth. But in reality, we're stuck surrounded by idiots, and about fifty guys who would all hit on her if given the chance.

I don't want anyone to have the chance. I want her to be mine.

"Let's go for a walk," I say.

She grins. "Sounds fun."

Then she turns, grabs the edge of the pool, and lifts herself out. I don't know if she means to put her incredibly sexy ass in my face or not, but I'm liking the view regardless.

I climb out and grab us both a towel from the stack of freshly laundered towels courtesy of Mindy's maid. They're huge and plush and I've taken more than one of these things home with me in the past.

Mindy's bartender stands behind a stone bar on the back patio. He offers Maddie a drink but she politely shakes her head. "No, thanks."

As much as I could use another beer to deal with how nervous this girl makes me, I follow her lead and decline a drink as well.

"You can drink if you want to," she says, looking back at me as we weave through a group of people.

"Nah, I'm good."

She considers this for a moment and then gives me a soft smile, tugging her towel closer around her. "So, where are we walking?"

I point toward the backyard. "There's a garden at the back of the property. It's nice at night."

Mindy's mom loves exotic gardens and has employed more than enough sexy gardeners over the years I've known her. Mindy and I always speculate that there's something going on between her mom and the gardeners, but we've never actually found evidence. One thing is for sure though; the garden is really nice. It has a paved walkway and little twinkle lights glowing everywhere.

"Oooh," Maddie says as we approach the glow at the front of the garden. Luckily, no one else is here since they'd all rather congregate at the pool. "This is kind of romantic."

"Romantic?" I say, putting a hand to my chest. "Are you trying to seduce me?"

I expect her to laugh or maybe pretend to gag or something.

Instead she wraps her hand around my arm and leans in, her wet air on my shoulder. "Maybe," she says, gazing up at the starry night sky. Then she lets go. "Maybe I'm still figuring it out."

It was only a few seconds, but my arm aches with the desire to touch her again. We turn around the corner where rose bushes fill the air with a fragrant scent. I try to sound confident. "What can I do to convince you?"

She stops walking. Tugs the towel around her shoulders and gazes up at me. "Why do you like me?"

"Is that a trick question?"

Okay, I probably shouldn't have said that, but it's the first thing I thought of.

She makes this noncommittal little shrug. "I just want to know."

"Well . . ." I begin. Maybe I'm just a d-bag controlled by his manhood, but the fact that she's so beautiful is the first answer that comes to mind. I know an answer like that will make me look shallow, so I take my time, trying to think of the perfect words to use.

Maddie frowns and looks at the fitness tracker watch on her wrist. "Crap," she says, eyes wide with fear. "I need to get my phone."

"Everything okay?"

"I don't know," she says, dropping the towel to the sidewalk as she takes off running toward the house.

I pick up her towel and jog along behind her. She goes inside, which is cold as hell when you're soaking wet, and grabs a small purse from the chaise lounge that's filled with purses.

"My mom texted me SOS," she says, frantically digging through her bag until she pulls out a cell phone. "I missed two calls from her earlier, but I didn't think it was anything important, ya know?" She shakes her head and chuckles sarcastically. "And here I thought my step-dad was dumb for getting me this silly waterproof watch thing."

"Let's go somewhere quieter," I say, pointing toward the front door. Even though most of the party goers are outside, there's still loud music pumping through the Carmichael's sound system.

I open the front door for her and we step into the warm night air. "Um, I can go if you want," I say, realizing I'm being a little too forward by sticking around.

"It's okay." She fumbles with her phone, frowning as she tries to work the unlock screen.

"Mom?" she says as soon as the call connects. She listens for a second and then says, "I'll be right there."

"Everything okay?" I ask.

She peers up at me, her face glowing from the porch light. She has a little freckle near her hairline, and her lips are still a little sparkly from her lip gloss, even though the rest of her makeup has washed away. Doesn't matter—she's beautiful without it.

"My little sister is sick," she says, gripping her phone tightly in her hands. "She's asking for me, because—well, she needs me." Maddie looks up to the sky and then back at me. "My mom used to work a lot, and so I always had to take care of Starla when she got sick."

"Want me to take you home?" I say, realizing a little too late that I walked here and don't have my car.

She shakes her head. "I'm just two houses over. I'll be fine."

Two houses over? As in, she lives in Shady Heights?

Uh oh. It feels like all of the air has been knocked out of my lungs. Of course she lives in Shady Heights. *Of course.* I already knew she was too good for me, and now here I am letting all of that get ruined as I flirt with her.

I swallow, and she touches my arm. "What's wrong?"

I force my frown into a smile. "Nothing. Just uh, just making sure you're okay." I run a hand through my hair, which is all wet, so it doesn't work as smoothly as I was expecting.

"Want me to walk you home? Make sure you get there safely?"

She glances toward the right, where I'm guessing her house is. "Yes."

We're halfway down Mindy's driveway when I realize how badly I've dug myself into a hole. Here I am totally falling for this girl when she is entirely too good for me. She'll figure it out soon enough. She'll want more, a guy who can give her the things she's used to. Fancy dates, expensive gifts. That's why Mindy was being so coy earlier today. Mindy knows better than to set me up with her new friend. She's like a sister to me, of course, but that doesn't change the fact that I am falling for a girl I'll never be able to have.

As we walk, Maddie tells me about her little sisters. One is almost five and one is two. I try not to listen too closely, because every detail I know about this girl is one more way I'll hurt when she ditches me.

Maybe that's the kind of thing Josh was talking about earlier. We're too young for real relationships, and everything we do now is just a big build up to a future heartbreak.

Hell, I can already feel my heart ripping in half, and all Maddie has given me is that drop dead gorgeous smile.

19

MADDIE

AND THAT'S when I wake up.

I can dream about hot guys all day long. I can pretend they're in my new room at Landon's house, all sexy and hot and into me. I can even practically feel what it would be like to kiss a guy.

But love?

Yeah, not happening. Even my sleep-deprived brain knows better than to go along with such a stupid dream like that one.

I groan and roll over, the soft sheets and comfy mattress once again reminding me how lucky I am to have my mom fall in love with Landon.

Last night was rough with poor Starla. She has a fever and a sore throat, which means it's probably strep. Mom's taking her to the doctor today, but as for last night, I was up until dawn with my sister.

When I finally open my eyes, my thoughts still on Colby, I look around and find that my room is spotless.

Pam's been here, probably while I was still asleep.

That is *so* weird.

Downstairs, my mom, sisters, and Landon are watching Disney Channel in the den. Mom's relaxing on the recliner, reading a magazine.

"Where's my sick girl?" I say, yawning.

"She's on her way to recovery," Landon says. He's wearing pajamas, matching pants and a shirt, which is something we've never worn in our lives. He and Starla are playing with a toy car that travels on a plastic track, both of them on the floor like kids.

"The doctor gave her some medicine," Mom says, looking up from her magazine. "Thank you so much for helping me with her last night, honey. I'm sorry you had to cut your party short."

Colby's face flashes in my mind.

"It's no problem," I say, ruffling Starla's hair before sitting on the couch. I pull a couch pillow into my lap. "Family first."

"Did you have fun?" Mom asks.

I nod. "Mindy was pretty nice, which is weird because she comes off as a stone cold bit—" I clamp my mouth shut since Emma is watching me. "Brat. But she was really nice last night. I guess it's because she thinks I'm one of them."

Landon nods in agreement at the same time Mom says, "No, that's not it. She just didn't know you before."

Landon and I exchange a look, and I think it's kind of cool that we have this secret together about me pretending to be a new person.

I shrug. "Anyway, I really liked her. And I haven't been in a swimming pool in forever, so that was fun."

"Good," Mom says. "Landon has saved us from a life of hell."

"Bad word!" Starla says, pointing her chubby little finger toward our mother.

"Oops!" Mom says, clamping a hand over her mouth.

Pam pokes her head into the movie room a few hours later. "Mindy Carmichael is here to see you, hun."

She steps out of the way, and Mindy enters looking like some kind of runway model. Her hair is long and wavy, her makeup gorgeous. She can really pull off a smoky eye, something I've never been able to do with the eye makeup I bought from the dollar store.

Even though she's one of the popular girls, she kind of has a gothic vibe about her. Like a preppy Wednesday Adams, which somehow makes her look even cooler than the rest of the popular crowd.

She's wearing combat boots with very short black shorts

and a purple flowy tank top with a long strand of pearls around her neck.

"Yeah so I totally didn't get your number last night," she says, plopping down in the recliner chair next to mine. "I had to come over uninvited like some freaking stalker."

I snort and grab the remote to pause my movie. My phone is in my chair's cup holder, so I get it out and slide open the lock screen. "What's your number? I don't have mine memorized yet."

"Girl, you're worse than I am," she says with a laugh. She tells me her number, which I type into my phone and then I call her so she'll have my new number. I had the old number memorized of course, but they don't let you keep the number from a prepaid cell phone when you switch to a real phone plan.

"So . . . I saw you walk off with Colby last night," she says, wiggling her eyebrows at me. "How'd that go?"

"It didn't." I've been watching this movie by myself since Starla is napping and Mom is baking cookies with Emma, but still, I look around the room anyway to make sure we're really alone. "Nothing happened."

Her face scrunches up. "*Wha?* He didn't make a move on you? I'm gonna kick his ass."

I shake my head. "He didn't have a chance to make a move. My mom called and I had to run home since my little sister was sick."

She lifts an eyebrow, and I get the feeling she doesn't really believe me, but she doesn't press any further.

"So . . . you still like him? Or you want me to find you someone better?"

"He's hot, Mindy." I'm glad the theater room is pretty dark so she can't see me blush. "How much better do you think I could do?"

She flips her hair and studies her nails. "Girl, you're almost as hot as I am—and I mean that in a good way. You could get any guy you want."

I snort. "I am not even close to being as hot as you are."

"Hello," she says, circling her fingers around her face. "I did not wake up like this. We just need to style you up right and you'll be bang-able in no time."

I've always been a low maintenance kind of girl, which I thought I liked. But really, I didn't wear makeup or dress nice because I couldn't afford to. And now that I have the means to make myself look better . . . I kind of want to do it. Does that make me shallow and pathetic?

I swallow. As much as I want to be a new person with this new change in my life, I also don't want to lose who I am at heart. I'm a good person who doesn't really care about super-ficial stuff.

But I also want Colby to like me.

I bite on my bottom lip. "Will you give me some pointers to look hotter? I want Colby to like me."

Her lips slide to the side of her mouth. "You know what, Maddie? I like you. You're not afraid to say what you want, and I think that's cool. It's also why the other M's don't like you, but screw them."

"Wait, what?" I sit up in my chair. "Maria and Matilda don't like me?"

She rolls her head in this nonchalant way. "They're just annoyed that you like Colby. I guess they've both been wanting to hook up with him this year?" She rolls her eyes. "I dunno. Those bitches say they're my best friends but then refuse to tell me they're crushing on a guy that's basically my *brother*. I mean, really?" She flicks her hand in the air. "Bitches. That's why I didn't invite them over today."

"I don't want to like him if it's going to start drama," I say. As quickly as I've been accepted into the M's, I could easily be kicked out.

Mindy shakes her head. "Screw them. Seriously. They had years to speak up and they never did."

She stands and gives me a look that could move mountains. "Colby Jensen is your man if you want him. Now come on."

My brows narrow. "Where are we going?"

"Uh, *shopping*," she says with a roll of her eyes. "You wanted to look hot, remember? Let's go."

I can't argue with that. We take her Lexus to the mall even though I kind of want to drive my new car. I've only driven it to the store twice since I got it because there's really no other places to go. Getting to drive to school on Monday is about the only reason I'm looking forward to returning to the world of higher education. But every other aspect of going back to school can go screw itself.

At the mall, Mindy drags me into stores I've never heard of, with price tags that make my eyes bug out. She grabs clothes off the rack like she's some kind of fashion expert— which I guess she is—and shoves me into a fitting room.

When I step out of the fitting room wearing a mini skirt and a tank top, Mindy is ready with her phone camera.

"Pose for me, gorgeous."

I don't know why I do it, but I find myself cocking out my leg, putting a hand on my hip and throwing a sexy wink to the camera.

"Perfect!" Mindy says, snapping more photos. I get all into it and make up silly poses, even turning to the side and poking out my butt, with a finger to my lips like I'm naughty Marilyn Monroe.

I buy everything Mindy picks out, swiping my credit card like I've been doing it my whole life. As soon as I sign the receipt, I get this sick feeling in my gut. Two hundred dollars would have fed us all for a month or more, back when we were poor. Now I'm dropping it on a pile of cotton and denim and chunky bracelets.

Still, I push the thoughts to the back of my mind and try to focus on the good parts of this. I have a friend, and I'm having fun. These kinds of things never happened before I become rich by association.

Mindy and I stop for a Starbucks, and this time I order the java chip frappuccino, acting like I know exactly what I'm doing at the counter even though this is only my second fancy coffee.

Mindy sips from her latte and checks her phone. A smirk slides across her lips and she looks up at me like she's holding back an epic secret.

"What?" I ask, my heart racing. For a split second, I fear that she's just realized who I am. A trailer trash fraud.

She turns her phone toward me, where I see Colby's name at the top of the text message screen.

I panic as I realize she's sent him two of the photos of me

pretending to be sexy in the fitting room. But then I panic even more when I read his reply.

Colby: Why waste your time giving her a makeover, Min? She was beautiful before.

"Oh my God, you didn't!" I shriek, grabbing her phone.

She laughs. "Oh, I did. But look how well it worked out for you."

I stare at the photos she sent him, at the sultry, sexy, and fearless girl on the screen. That girl is so not me. I only posed like that because I was being dorky, yet somehow they look . . . good.

I have never been so embarrassed and strangely proud in my life.

I groan and give her phone back. "I am gonna die."

"Noooo," she says, putting an arm around me. "I know I ragged on him last night, but Colby is a good guy." She looks up and nods her head like she's thinking it over. "I mean, he's boring, and he's kinda—well, boring—but he's a good guy. He's never been into slutty girls, if you know what I mean. So you're kind of perfect for him. It's just gross because, like I said, he's like my brother. So yeah. Gross."

"Well he's not *my* brother," I say.

"True." She thumbs through her phone. "What's your Instagram? We gotta post these."

"My what?"

The second I say it, I know I've screwed up. Mindy gives

me a sideways glance. "Instagram? The app? On your phone?"

"Oh," I say with a nod, as I proceed to bullshit my way out of this. I have no idea what Instagram is, but I pretend I do. "New phone, remember? I haven't set it up yet."

"Ah, well let's do that, shall we?"

20

———

COLBY

WITH ONLY TWO days left before school starts, the guys and I have decided to take it easy and just chill out a bit. That means we ordered a pizza, played a ton of video games, and then came out to Josh's pool.

I'm still kicking myself for not getting Maddie's number, especially since we had a few awesome moments together. She certainly seemed like she liked me, but maybe she was just being nice.

If I know anything about Mindy, my old friend has probably convinced Maddie to scope out all the eligible guys to date before she settles on me. This makes an annoyed type of anger rise up in my chest. I love Mindy, I do, but the girl can be brutal when it comes to dating. I kind of wish she'd never have met Maddie so she wouldn't be so influential on her.

Still, school starts soon, and I'll see Maddie then. I promised to show her around and she seemed to agree to that, right? I'll get her number in two days when we're walking to first period together. I'll do whatever it takes to win her over. I don't care how hard it is.

And yeah, the smart, logical part of my brain knows this little flirty thing we have might end before it even begins, but that's a chance I'm willing to take.

"Any more matches?" Josh asks. He's sitting in the shallow end of his pool, his back up against one of the jets.

"Matches?" I ask, looking over at him. It's hot as hell outside, so we haven't started a fire in the fire pit or anything. I've actually stolen his little sister's hot pink donut floaty and have my arms slung over the edges to hold me up in the water because it's too hot to be out of the pool.

"On the dating app." Josh answers.

"Dude," Bryce says from the edge of the pool. He's still eating the last slice of pizza, so he's only sitting with his feet in the water. "I got twenty-two likes overnight. Some of them are pretty hot, too."

"But have you actually met up with these girls?" I ask.

Bryce nods. "Hell yeah. I'm meeting one tonight. Hooking up is so much easier with this app. You don't have to talk and get to know each other and all that mess."

I shake my head. "You need to get checked for STDs, man."

Bryce simply kicks the water, sending a splash of chlorine right in my face. He snorts and keeps eating his pizza.

I look at Josh. "I uninstalled it. Everyone was too old, too weird, or too far away."

Josh makes this *pshh* sound. "You didn't give it enough time, dumbass."

I shrug. "I'll stick to girls I meet in real life."

Josh had been wrapped up in a game of beer pong when I walked with Maddie in the garden. I'm pretty sure he didn't see any of it, or he would have already asked me about her. Bryce didn't show up until an hour later, sparing me the competition. Hitting on hot new girls is kind of his hidden talent.

The sound of the back door opening makes us all look over. Abigail, Josh's thirteen-year-old sister walks out wearing a bathing suit that's entirely too skimpy for a little kid her age.

"Hey guys," she says, throwing her hair over her shoulder. "What's up?"

"Go away, Abby," Josh says, waving her away with his hand.

"Screw you, Josh. I can be here if I want, it's my house too."

"I can't wait until I move out," Josh groans, throwing his head back. "I'm sick of little kids everywhere."

"Whatever," Abigail mutters. She flashes me a smile and then saunters over to the pool's edge. It's no secret she has a huge crush on all of Josh's friends, so I have to balance this thin line of being nice to her because she's a kid, and making sure I'm not so nice as to make her think I'd like her back. Unfortunately, she seems to take even a contrite look to be some hidden sign that you're into her. It's very annoying.

After only a few minutes of Abigail laying out on a beach towel, Josh decides he's sick of being around his little sister and insists that we go inside.

It's already been an hour since we last ate, so I'm already hungry again. "Should we get some more food?" I ask, toweling off my hair as I plop down on Josh's bed. "I could go for Chinese food."

Josh looks like he's about to agree when Bryce whoops from across the room.

"Da-*amn*," he says to his phone screen. "Mindy posted pictures of this new chick who just moved here. She's hot as hell."

My stomach launches up into my throat. The last thing I need is for Bryce to start hitting on Maddie.

He clutches his phone to his chest and closes his eyes. "Oh, Instagram, you have been good to me."

I breathe a little sigh of relief. Although Mindy posted a couple photos she captioned as "sexy clothes shopping with my new M", she didn't tag Maddie in them. I may or may not (okay I did) spend a few hours searching for her name on both Instagram and Snapchat and Twitter. Maddie either doesn't have any social media profiles, or she has them severely privacy blocked. Probably the latter, obviously. No one our age isn't on social media.

It just sucks because I don't have her number and I couldn't find her online. I've debated asking Mindy for it, but then she'd no doubt take all the credit for hooking us up. I learned a long time ago that one thing you should always try to avoid is being in Mindy Carmichael's debt, real or imagined.

That girl can tell you it's hot outside and then take the credit for it when you agree with her and put on a pair of sunglasses.

"She's hot, but she's unavailable," I say. I don't know why I do it. The very sentence alone opens me up for follow up questions—all of which will have to be a lie since the original thing was a lie.

But the thought of Bryce setting his sights on the new girl before I've officially won her over makes my blood boil. I don't know how he does it, but Bryce has a silver tongue that's a force to be reckoned with.

You know when you hear those stories on the news about a teacher hooking up with a fourteen-year-old student? Bryce does crap like that. He's never been caught, either.

Sure, he's tall, dark, handsome and all that, and girls think he's awesome, but he's kind of a sleazebag when it comes to dating. I meant it about the STD thing. I don't even drink after the guy. He's been having sex since he was thirteen years old and Josh and I still thought girls had cooties.

He will *not* get to Maddie.

Even if I don't deserve a girl like her, that won't stop me from protecting her from a guy like him.

Josh turns on an action movie, something I don't really pay attention to because Bryce keeps verbally commenting on Instagram photos of hot girls at our school. I keep waiting for him to mention Maddie again, or maybe even for him to call Mindy and ask about her.

To my relief, he doesn't. That doesn't mean he won't still try to hook up with her. It just means that for now, Maddie is safe from his prying, womanizing claws.

21
______

MADDIE

THE FOOD COURT at any mall is a paradise of delicious and unhealthy foods. Cheese fries, corn dogs, tacos, pizza. Ice cream and cookie cakes.

But here I am eating a salad.

This is my life now, as a popular girl. Mindy told me that this place called Salata—a mall food place I had until now always ignored—was the best salad joint ever. She said it like there are no other food options in the mall, and that's when I realized that popular girls also = skinny, and skinny = salads.

Which really sucks because I'm thin from years of being poor, not years of trying to be thin. I've kind of enjoyed eating a ton of food lately.

Anyhow, we're having a salad. And it is pretty good, as far as salads go, but when a kid walks by with a tray of cheesy fries, it takes all of my willpower not to trample him and steal his food.

Another new addition to my life is the app Instagram. I always knew my fellow classmates are addicted to social media, but having no internet connection, no computer, and no smartphone for the last few years has left me in the dark. Now I understand it.

Mindy didn't ask too many questions when I lied and said I didn't have an account already because "my old life sucked and I deleted it to get away from it." I guess that kind of thing made sense to her because she just nodded in agreement and helped me create a new account. Now it's filled with pictures of Mindy and me lounging by the pool, hanging out in my new movie theater room, painting our nails—you get the idea.

Now I'm following Mindy's lead and snapping a photo of my salad for the whole world to see. So far I have twelve followers, mostly guys, and all of them Mindy's friends.

Colby is missing from that list.

I didn't seek him out online last night, even though I wanted to. I guess I want him to find me online and add me first.

It all sounds so dumb when I think about it, but it would still mean a lot to me if Colby followed me first.

I stab my fork into a piece of cucumber. "So, how long does it take to get followers around here?" I ask, trying to sound casual. "I noticed you have two thousand."

Mindy nods. "The secret is posting half-naked selfies, to be honest."

I nearly choke on my salad. Mindy laughs. "But if you mean people from our school . . . particularly a certain boy . . ."

I roll my eyes, again, trying to be somewhat nonchalant

about the whole thing. "I would like to meet more school people, I guess. I mean, I'm new here and all."

Mindy nods, setting down her fork like she's got the perfect plan. "I got you."

She holds up her phone, the camera facing me, and says, "Look sexy."

I lift an eyebrow, confused as to how I'm supposed to look sexy with a bite of salad in my mouth.

Mindy laughs, snaps a photo, and then looks down at her phone. "Perfect."

I lean forward, but I can't see what she's doing over the booth. She holds up a finger to me while she types something one-handed on her phone.

"Okay. Done."

I go to Instagram on my own phone. Mindy just posted the picture of me, fork in hand, eyebrow lifted. I guess it's kind of cute, but definitely not sexy.

The caption reads:

Hey, bitches. Go follow my new BFF Maddie Sinclair!

My phone immediately gets notifications that I have new followers. Matilda and Maria follow me, and even like some of my posts, which is encouraging because I don't think they exactly like me. This is now the second time Mindy has come over to hang out without inviting them.

"Look, now you're at twenty-five followers and all you

had to do was eat some salad," Mindy says, sipping from her unsweetened tea.

"Well, it helps that I got a shout out from you."

She looks up and makes this little fake bashful smile. "That's what I'm here for."

I scroll through the ever-growing list of my new followers. So far, it's a bunch of popular people I recognize as the students who totally ignored me before Spring Break. There's a few others, too. People I don't recognize, and people from exotic locations that are far better than Louetta, TX. The exotic location followers are mostly guys, and I'm guessing those are Mindy's friends obtained through posting half-naked photos.

I try not to get my hopes up, especially during these few minutes while we're eating lunch, because not everyone is on their phone all the time. I barely saw Colby with his phone, so he's probably not even checking Instagram right now, right?

So that's why he hasn't followed me. I tell myself to get it together and forget about him until he decides to seek me out. It's exactly what Mindy would do. It's exactly what any self-respecting woman would do.

At least, I think so.

So we finish our shopping, and after buying a few more outfits and then stopping for a healthy smoothie that tastes like strawberries mixed with dirt, I have two hundred and forty new followers, but none of them are Colby.

And then, finally, at eight-thirteen in the evening, Colby Jensen follows me.

Colby's Instagram isn't exactly what I would have pictured. Of course, until a couple of days ago, I'd never seen the app so I guess I don't have much experience in the matter of what teenage guys' social media profiles look like.

His username isn't Colby, but HotRodLife99, and his user picture is of him and another guy, someone I think is on the football team. This guy is tall and lean and has a smirk that's practically screaming "don't trust me."

Colby's pictures are posted every couple of weeks. There's some classic cars, new cars, and basically, a lot of cars. And then photos of him with his friends, either at parties, the beach, or the pool. There's also a lot of pictures of some place that looks like a nightclub. The main thing my prying eyes look for isn't there.

Pictures of Colby with another girl. It's a relief, even though I was pretty sure he didn't have a girlfriend since he was flirting with me.

Colby likes all seventeen of my pictures and comments on a few of them, telling me how cute I look.

I'm practically floating all night. I only come back to reality when Starla, who's still a little sick, comes padding into my room after ten o'clock, a stuffed bunny rabbit under her arm.

"You okay?" I ask, climbing off my bed to kneel down to her level.

She shakes her head, holding up her arms to me.

I press the back of my hand to her forehead, but her fever is gone, thanks to the medicine. In our old house, Starla would always crawl into bed with me. I pick her up and put her on my bed, then line a bunch of pillows along the other side so she can't roll off.

I'm still up watching TV, so I'll wait until she falls asleep to carry her back to her room.

Once she's snuggled up in my ridiculous amount of pillows, she settles down, closing her eyes. I sit cross-legged in the middle of my bed, the room lit up from the soft glow of my television, while I stare at Instagram.

I get a new direct message from HotRodLife99.

Okay, I didn't even know direct messaging was a thing, but now my heart leaps into my throat.

I read the message with trembling fingers.

Hey there. You awake?

Yep. It's not that late, lol

Cool. So will I see you when school starts back?

I hope so

Me too

I bite my lip so hard it goes numb, but I can't help myself. At last, after hours of daydreaming about this boy, we're finally talking.

Before I know it, it's already past midnight, and we've been texting back and forth through this app all night long. He's hitting on me pretty strongly, which would be a turn off, but I'm trying to go with it. Just because I'm not used to this kind of attention doesn't mean it's not normal. Popular girls probably deal with it all the time.

And now I'm one of them.

I fall asleep clutching my phone, smiling like an idiot, and daydreaming about how cute Colby Jensen looks in swim trunks.

22

COLBY

THE ONLY THING that can really ruin a night of relaxing is Greg showing up with his dumb girlfriend.

They're both away at college, and now that he's in his first year of graduate school, we hardly ever see him. Which was fine with me. Random texts and social media convos with my brother is really all the interaction I need with the guy who always has to find a way to remind me that he's so much better than I am.

But now he's here, and so is Mayra. My brother's longtime girlfriend is tall, thin, and has a face that looks like a bossy bitch. Luckily for her, she *is* a bossy bitch so her looks suit her perfectly. She's a med student studying to become a surgeon, and my parents act as if that alone makes her perfect enough to be sainted.

I was really counting on chilling at home all day, maybe hitting up the park to play some basketball or something. But now I have to be in family entertainment mode.

Mom and Dad freak out when Greg and Mayra arrive,

and Mom immediately insists that we all go out to dinner tonight. Never mind the fact that just thirty minutes ago, I overheard them arguing about which payment to let lapse this month until Dad gets paid again. Let's go out to eat somewhere fancy! Makes total sense.

We end up at Landry's, an overpriced, overhyped seafood restaurant that my parents can't afford. I try to order the cheapest thing on the menu, but even that is so pricey it makes my insides hurt.

The only thing worse than suffering through a pointless dinner with my family and listening to my brother talk about how great he is, is knowing that the bill is going to be the source of my parents' future arguments.

Again, I think about finding my own job and taking over the payments on my car and insurance, whether they like it or not. One thing is for sure though: I will never be like my parents when it comes to money.

Thinking about money makes me think of Maddie, but it's not like I'm not already thinking about her. Yesterday was agony having to listen to Bryce go on and on about how hot she is. I tried acting like it was no big deal, but the truth is, I can't let him know I'm crushing on her. He'd only take that as an invitation to compete with me for Maddie's heart.

Here's the thing: even if Maddie was some horrible person and I hated her, I still wouldn't let her date Bryce. He's not exactly good to girls in any possible way.

After dinner, we head home and my family piles onto the couches in the den to keep up the conversation about how great and wonderful and perfect the eldest Jenson son is. I excuse myself, making up a phony story about how my stomach hurts.

No one seems to care.

I slip into my room, take a hot shower, and then crash on my bed to watch TV. Maddie, an ever-present person in my mind, seems to have gotten even more beautiful with each day I think about her.

I check Instagram, scrolling through my friend's stupid photos of their Spring Breaks. Some of them went on vacation to Jamaica, Hawaii, Florida and the likes. I hate all of them just on principle. My family hasn't had a real vacation in years, but I hope to save up to take my own trip once I graduate high school next year.

I'm lazily scrolling through my picture feed when I see that pink hair. Mindy posted a photo of Maddie eating a salad. Wow, even doing something boring looks good on her.

I click on her profile, excited that I finally found her on social media. She only has a few photos, but they're all super adorable.

I'm sitting here grinning like some kind of lovesick idiot for over an hour when I finally get the balls to click the follow button.

With any luck, she'll follow me back.

23

———

MADDIE

EVEN WHEN I'M all alone in my room—well, besides Starla sleeping next to me—I blush from head to toes when I get Colby's message.

———

Would you like to go on a date with me?

———

I suck in a quick breath of air, and smile so big my face might rip in half. We've been chatting online for hours now, and he finally asked the big question. Of course, now that I've gotten to know Colby a bit, I'm not entirely sure I want to go out with him.

Yes, he's super cute, and yes, he seemed great at Mindy's party. But online he's kind of . . . a little perverted, I guess. Maybe that's just how guys are.

At first, he asked me to send him a picture via the direct

message feature. I told him there were pictures of me on my Instagram feed already so what would be the point?

Of course, he didn't want one of those pictures.

He wanted a picture that I couldn't show the general public.

And let's be honest here, I guess that's how guys are and everything, but it really hurt my feelings. Here I was thinking we were making a connection, getting to know each other more to see if we could really have something between us or if it was just a stupid crush. He kind of ruined all of the sweetness points he earned by walking me home after Mindy's party. In just one winky faced emoji message, he made me feel like a piece of meat.

Since I'm not ready to take a revealing photo of myself at the moment, or maybe not ever, I lied and told him I was stuck with lots of people over and couldn't escape to take a photo. Plus, I then tried to give him a way to get back on my good side by telling him he should wait until we know each other better to ask for that kind of thing.

That's what made him ask me on a date. And yeah, I guess the few lewd things he's said before he asked for this date are kind of disappointing, but at least he still wants to go out. Maybe he's just messing around? I don't know. I've heard people say you can't really tell what a person means by reading text. It's devoid of any emotion or facial expressions. Maybe the whole thing was just a joke.

I'm trying to figure out how to word my reply, and it's taking a while. I mean, I could say YES and add in a smiley face for good measure, but I want to play this cool. I try to think of what Mindy would do, and I even consider texting her for some advice. But then she might show up at my door, at ten o'clock at night, and I don't want to explain that to my mom.

After what feels like forever, but really only lasts a few minutes, I come up with this reply:

Hmm, I'll have to check my schedule.

My finger hovers over the send button. Then my phone gets a new notification. It's from Instagram.

Colby Jensen just followed you.

Um, what? Ice fills my veins as I click on the profile of the person who just followed me. Their name is Colby. Their user photo is of Colby. I skim through a few dozen photos and they're all either Colby, Colby with friends, or a cute little dog named Gig. I swallow.

If this is Colby . . . who have I been talking to all night?

While my notifications bar fills up with this new Colby Jensen liking all of my photos, I go back to HotRodLife99 and look at his user picture. It's Colby standing next to a guy with black hair. I go back to the Colby Jensen profile and search through the pictures, not even taking time to realize there's no girl pictures on there. I find the same dark haired guy and click on the picture.

It's the guy eating a cheeseburger and the caption reads:

Bryce ate this whole thing in two minutes. #gross

Bryce?
Oh, no.
I follow Colby Jensen back and send him a DM.

Who is this?

Um, it's me? Colby?

The guy who walked me home from Mindy's party?

The very same

So . . . we haven't been chatting online for hours?

No?

Um, this sucks.

What happened?

HotRodLife99 has been messaging me all night and I thought it was you . . .

Can you meet me in the park between the Shady Heights and Shady Grove neighborhoods? In like five minutes?

I glance at the time on my phone and then type a reply before I can chicken out.

Yes.

With my heart pounding, I carry a sleeping Starla to her room and then quietly slip out. I put on some flip-flops and decide that five minutes isn't enough time to get dressed up for Colby, so I just go as I am, in pajamas with my hair in a messy bun. My mom is with Landon in their bedroom, and Pam has already gone to bed in her room down the hall, so I grab my car keys, which also has a house key, and slip out of the front door, locking it behind me.

Then I walk on foot toward the neighborhood park that separates my street from Colby's. It won't take long to walk there, and I don't want to risk waking up my mom by opening the garage door to get my car.

I hug my phone tightly in my hand, my car keys in the other as I walk toward the park. Heat rushes to my cheeks as I think about the entire conversation I just had with a guy who wasn't Colby.

Street lamps light up the park and I see Colby standing there when I'm still several yards away. He's wearing black basketball shorts and a white T-shirt that hugs tightly to his chest and arms. Messy dirty blonde hair that's nearly to his shoulders practically begs me to run my hands through it.

Instead, I stay calm and act like this isn't a big deal. Colby grins, his lips spreading into the cutest freaking smirk I've ever seen as I approach him.

"Hey," he says, his eyes sliding down to take in my outfit for a split second before they meet mine again. "Cute pajamas."

"Shut up," I say, hugging my arms around myself. I'm wearing a black tank top with little cats all over it, and matching pink shorts with flip-flops.

The way he looks at me makes me feel weightless, like a gentle wind could sweep me away forever.

Colby moves toward a bench and sits, motioning for me to join him. I sit on the opposite side, ignoring my body's urge to sit right up next to him.

"So what's going on with Bryce?" he asks, tucking his hair behind his ears.

I blow out a deep breath and gaze out at the empty swing set in the distance. "Oh my God, I don't even know. I'm so embarrassed."

He chuckles. "Honestly, I was hoping you wouldn't meet him for a while. He can be . . . intense, with pretty girls."

There he goes again, slipping compliments into everyday conversation like it's nothing. I bite my lip, wanting to tell him everything. Suddenly I'm so embarrassed I could cry.

"Well, he messaged me earlier, and I thought he was you," I say, covering my face with my hand. "This is so embarrassing."

"You didn't immediately know it wasn't me?" he says with a laugh. "I can't imagine that Bryce and I sound anything alike."

"He did sound kind of pushy," I admit with a sigh. "But here's the thing: I kind of flirted with him all night." I say it quickly just to get it out, and it ends up coming out like a question.

Colby's eyes widen for a second and then that grin reappears on his face. "What did you say?"

I hold out my phone for him, showing him the very long DM chain. His gorgeous face glows in the phone screen for a few seconds while he scrolls through it all.

"He asked you for *what?*" Colby says, a look of rage flashing across his face. "Wow, I'm glad you didn't comply."

I let out a huff of air. "I'm not slutty, Colby. I mean, I like you, but I'm not about to send some dirty photo that can be spread all around school."

His lips slide to the side of his mouth and he peers up at me for a long moment. Then he hands me back my phone, his fingers touching mine during the exchange.

"I didn't check my phone all day, or I would have followed you sooner," he says. "Sorry about Bryce. He's an idiot and he'll hit on every beautiful girl, hoping one of them will agree to go out with him."

"Well I was about to agree to his freaking date question before I realized it wasn't you!" My chest rises as I breathe in deeply. Embarrassment creeps over me. "I can't believe it. What am I supposed to do now?"

He scratches his neck. I catch the scent of some kind of boyish soap and it makes me want to nuzzle up against him. "Well, do you like him?"

"No," I say immediately. My lip curls. "Ew. No. I don't."

His voice gets lower. "Do you like anyone?"

I roll my eyes. "You know the answer to that, stupid."

His hand stretches across the back of the park bench. Though we're on opposite sides of it, we're both facing each other, our knees not that far apart. He lifts his fingers and pokes my shoulder, his touch sending an electric tingle down my arm.

"I think I know how you can fix this situation with Bryce," he says, never taking his eyes off me."

I put a finger to my lips, like I'm thinking. "Tell him the truth?"

Colby winces playfully and shakes his head. "Nope, I have a much better idea."

He takes out his phone and then slides closer to me on the bench, his arm seamlessly sliding around my shoulders. He turns on the camera on his phone, holds his hand up in front of us, and then leans in. My whole body warms as he gets closer, closer, closer, until his lips press against my forehead. The camera shutter sound plays, and then Colby lowers his phone so we can see it.

There I am, looking absolutely lovesick and wrapped in Colby's arms. I'm looking up at him, a grin on my face. Colby's eyes are closed, his lips pressed to my forehead.

My stomach flips over at how adorable the picture looks, even though I'm not even wearing makeup or anything. The look on my face, one of absolute bliss, really makes the whole photo.

He sends it to his Instagram account and has to remove his arm from around my shoulder to use both of his hands to type out a caption. It's worth it though, because what he writes is absolutely flawless.

Spending time with my new girl. #perfect

24

COLBY

MADDIE LETS me read her conversation with Bryce. The perverted stuff he told her makes my blood boil, and seeing her sending flirty things does all kinds of trauma to my heart. But knowing she sent those things thinking she was talking to me makes me feel awesome inside.

"I'm sorry for Bryce," I say, sliding my finger down her shoulder. My arm is slung across the back of this park bench, and my fingers are only close enough to graze her skin, although I'd like to do much more. "He can be a total jerk to girls."

A breeze sends Maddie's hair flying, and she tucks it behind her ears. "Are you saying that because you aren't the same way?"

I scoff. "No way, I'm not like him at all."

She leans forward, the moonlight making her look like an angel. "What are you like?"

"Well, for starters, I wouldn't have chatted with you on

Instagram all night. I'd have asked for your number and called you."

"Called me?" she says, and I swear she's flirting with me a little more than usual. "Do people call each other anymore? I thought it was all text."

I shrug. "When I like a girl, I'd rather hear her voice."

Her cheeks turn as pink as her hair, and she drops her face into her hands. "Well, I feel like a total idiot now."

"Aww, don't worry about it," I say, sliding a little closer to her. Our knees touch, my skin getting warm at the idea of being close to her. "Bryce will see the picture of us and know to back the hell off. Trust me."

She lifts up, looking at me with eager eyes. "You sure about that?"

I nod. "It's a best friend thing. He wanted you, but I just proved I got you first."

There's a flash of something in her eyes and I realize what that just sounded like, so I hold up my hand. "Not that you're property or anything, I swear. I'm a respectful guy. It's just that he wouldn't have stopped trying to date you unless he knew you were already into someone else."

I can't quite decipher her expression, but I don't think she's not hating me right now. I try to look confident, but I'm pretty sure it comes out bashful. "If you don't *really* like me, it's okay. I mean, I'd understand."

"I can't believe you kissed me," she says, a grin sliding across her lips. "I mean, it was on the forehead, but still."

"Does that mean you like me?" I ask, leaning a little bit closer to her.

Her eyes flit up toward mine. My entire body is buzzing

with how much I like this girl. We gaze at each other for so long, and her answer seems to take forever, but when she finally speaks I've nearly forgotten the question.

"I think I do," she says.

And then I kiss her.

Her lips are soft, and they tremble a little, but I think it's because she's nervous. I try to pull away, but she leans in closer, her hand grabbing my leg. I wrap my arms around her and pull her close, placing another kiss on her lips. This time, she kisses me back, grabs my shoulder and pulls me in.

Soon we're all over each other, and I can't even focus on breathing, much less my surroundings. All I know is her, the soft lavender smell of her shampoo, and the wonderful taste of her mouth on mine.

When we pull apart slightly, I run my thumb down her cheek.

"Want to come hang out at my house?" I ask, my voice barely a whisper.

She bites on her bottom lip. "Yes, but . . . only for a little bit."

I rise from the bench and reach for her hand, which slips so effortlessly into mine, you'd think our hands were made for each other.

And I don't even care how dumb that might sound, or how much my friends would rag on me for thinking that way. Maddie Sinclair is beautiful and kind and I really want her to be my girlfriend.

So I should probably do this perfectly right.

We walk the short distance to my house, and although I'm a little weirded out letting her see my place, when it's only a fraction of the size of her mansion, she doesn't seem to care about it. I'll make sure to take her out on a nice date soon. That way she can see I'm the right guy for her. One who can provide just like her own parents do.

"We'll go in the back door," I say. "It's the farthest away from my parents' room."

"Sneaky," Maddie says, wiggling her eyebrows.

"They probably wouldn't care if I had someone over," I say. "But since they're asleep, it's better to just sneak in."

She squeezes my hand and leans into me, her other arm grabbing my elbow. "I like you."

I kiss the top of her head. "I like you."

In the hallway, I twirl my hand toward my closed bedroom door. "Here it is," I whisper, making a grand gesture of opening the door.

"Hmm," she says, stepping into my room. "It's clean. That's nice."

"I'm a clean guy," I say, closing my door behind me. It's the truth, even if it's hard to believe. I prefer to keep my stuff tidy and organized. I can't stand being in Bryce's rotting dumpster of a bedroom. Josh's room isn't too bad, but he leaves dirty clothes all over the place.

I lean against my closed door while Maddie walks around my room, her expression curious and playful. "Nice photo," she says, touching the frame of a five-year-old me standing next to Mickey Mouse.

"So, now that you've seen my room, has your opinion of me changed?"

She turns toward me. "Yep."

"Good or bad?"

Her eyes narrow in this ridiculously sexy way, and she crosses the room until she's standing right in front of me. She lifts up on her toes and kisses me. "Good," she says.

I slide my arms over her hips and pull her close to me, our bodies pressing against each other in a way that makes my chest constrict.

"I'm nervous," she whispers, her lips near my collarbone.

"We don't have to do anything," I whisper back, running a hand through her pink hair. And unlike some of my friends, I truly mean it. "I just want to be around you for as long as you'll have me."

She rests her head on my shoulder and lets out a long breath. "Thank you."

25

MADDIE

AS MUCH AS I love my new car, riding to school with Colby is a million times better than driving myself. He drives a BMW, which is pretty nice and smells like his body wash. I'm pretty sure I can never get tired of the smell of him.

"So, was it as terrible as you imagined?" Colby asks as he circles through our long driveway, headed toward the gate which is still open from when I let him in.

"Yes," I say, exaggerating the word, but I can't hold back my grin. "It was terrible. I told them my friend was taking me to school and they wanted to know all about you."

Colby laughs. When he'd offered to drive me to school last night, I told him I didn't want to freak out my mom, but ultimately I'd decided to do it anyway. I mean, who wouldn't want to ride to school with Colby Jensen?

The truth is, she wasn't that freaked out. She assumed I meant Mindy when I said "friend" and when I corrected her and said it was a guy friend, she just gave me this little knowing smirk. I really hate that she was right on that one—there really is a reason to smirk about Colby.

I am totally into him.

It's a short drive to school, and I have a blast the entire time, until we pull into the parking lot. Suddenly, every nerve in my body twists into anxiety and panic.

This is my big debut as a new person. Sure, I have a few Instagram friends and Mindy has welcomed me into her clan of girls with M names, but this is school. Real school. The same school I've been attending invisibly for four months.

My stomach twists into knots. Colby pulls into a parking spot and cuts the engine. He grabs his backpack from the backseat and then flashes me that sexy smile of his. "You ready?"

I gulp. "Mhm, yeah." It doesn't sound nearly as confident as I'd hoped.

"So I'll take you to the office to get your schedule," he says, walking around to meet me at the front of his car.

Oh crap.

"I already have my schedule," I say quickly. "I, um, got it before Spring Break."

"Cool, where is it?" he asks, slinging his backpack over his shoulder. "Maybe we have a class together."

I already know we don't have any classes together. My lies expand into more lies as I try to keep up this façade that I'm an actual new girl. "I forgot to bring it, but I memorized the schedule, so it's no big deal."

Colby quirks an eyebrow at me, but then he reaches for my hand and I take it, nearly forgetting every single thought in my head.

I love the way my hand fits into his.

"So what do you have first?" he asks.

"US History, then Chemistry, then Algebra two," I say, holding up fingers as I count them off. "Then childcare for fourth period, which I'm pretty sure you're probably not in . . ." I say with a laugh.

Colby shakes his head. "Nope."

I grin. "Then I have lunch, then childcare again since it's a split class, then gym."

"Damn, we don't have any classes together," he says with a sigh. "But I have C lunch as well, so I'll see you there."

"Cool," I say. I usually eat lunch alone on the long bench outside of the library, but I know exactly where the football players and the M's sit at lunch. It's the envied area of the cafeteria, and today I'll get to sit there.

My stomach feels all fluttery at the thought of it.

Colby walks me to my US History class, never letting go of my hand until the very last second. I am on cloud freaking nine, practically bouncing all over the place with my excitement. I can tell people are noticing me for the first time by their curious looks, or double takes when they see me with Colby. It's not like what I'd imagined in my dreams, though. Nothing like those movies or TV shows where a new girl arrives and everyone seems to stop, the world slows, and all eyes turn to the new girl.

It's definitely not like that.

But my world sure stops when Colby gives me a quick kiss on the lips before going to his own first period class. I sink into my desk with a sigh. My new life is perfect.

I have a close call in third period. For the first two classes, a few people talked to me, said they saw me on Instagram, and were generally nice.

But in third period, my teacher called me up to her desk and said she never got admission information for a new student. My heart thudded like crazy, but I quietly explained that it's me, the same Maddie Sinclair that's been in her class for four months, and that only my hair color was different. She laughed and apologized for not recognizing me.

The rest of the day goes smoothly. Colby finds me before lunch and we sit together. Although now I have enough money to buy a real meal from the cafeteria, I can barely eat any of it because I'm so excited to be here, with the M's and with Colby sitting so close to me that our legs are touching.

Everything is nearly perfect. Matilda has a new boyfriend, so although she's sitting with us at lunch, she's mostly absorbed in him. Maria hangs out with us, but she's still kind of cold toward me. Mindy makes up for it though, by being as friendly as if she's known me her whole life.

Soon, we slip into a normal routine. Colby drives me to school, we hold hands and share food at lunch, Maria gives me the stink eye but Mindy treats me like her favorite.

An entire week passes before I even realize it. Time really does go by faster when you're popular. By Friday, I have two hundred Instagram followers, and a few friends in every single class.

For as good as it feels to be noticed, I also struggle with the weight of how unfair life can be. In every single class, not one person mentions the girl who used to sit in the desk I sit in now. Not one person notices that I am the same person, the same student who was here all along. It's as if the old Maddie just disappeared without a trace and no one cares at all.

26

COLBY

AFTER ANOTHER DAY of mowing Mrs. Ruiz's lawn, and two more days of my dad dropping money in front of me, saying he's doing just fine at work and I should go out and have fun, I finally have enough cash to take Maddie out somewhere nice. We've been getting to know each other all this week, but since I'm in all AP classes, I've had homework after homework keeping me busy at night.

We've only seen each other once after school, and our make out session, while nice, only lasted ten minutes. I am dying to spend more quality time with this girl outside of school. She's still not totally comfortable introducing me to her family just yet, so that doesn't give us many options since when she comes to my house, it can be guaranteed that Josh or Bryce, or both will show up.

I have learned a lot more about her in this past week together. Like how her mom just got engaged to Landon, so he isn't her official step-dad yet. Maddie has been helping her mom plan the wedding, which happens in two weeks.

Maddie hasn't invited me to be her date to the event, but I'm trying not to hint at it or anything. If she's not comfortable introducing me to her family, I just need to wait until she is.

Which is also partly why I want to take her on this date. We see each other at school, text and talk all night, and hold hands every chance we get. But it's not enough. I'm not ready to settle down into some stupid high school relationship. I want magic, sparks, all of that stuff I previously thought was kind of lame. I want it all, and I want it with Maddie.

She answers the phone on Saturday morning with a groggy rasp to her voice.

"Did I wake you?" I ask, holding the phone to my ear while I lay in bed staring at my ceiling.

"No," she says, just before breaking into a yawn. "Okay, maybe a little bit."

"Sorry. I should have texted first."

"No, you can always call. I like it."

This makes me smile. I grip the phone tighter and close my eyes, wishing that she were here next to me.

"So I was thinking, if you're free tonight . . . maybe you'd like to go on a date with me?"

"A date?" she says in this funny voice. "Like, a real, genuine, *date?*"

"Yes ma'am." I'm pretty sure she'll say yes, but I'm holding my breath anyhow. The two seconds it takes her to reply feels like an eternity.

"That sounds fun," she finally says. "Where do you want to go?"

"It's a surprise," I say, feeling a rush of excitement run through my veins. "But I'll pick you up around six, okay?"

"Awesome," Maddie says, yawning again. "I'm gonna go back to sleep for a few hours and then it'll be date time."

I glance over at the clock and realize it's still seven hours until date time. She's lucky if she can sleep, because I'll be anxiously planning this date until I go pick her up. "See you then."

I'm so nervous I could throw up. I need this date to go well, so I've psyched myself out over it. My injured knee is aching, probably from all the stress. When Mom hears me cursing over the ironing board, she puts her hands on her hips and gives me a once over.

"What's going on with you?" she asks.

I let out a frustrated sigh and sit the iron up on the board. "I can't get this freaking shirt to look good."

"Since when do you wear button-up shirts anyhow?" she says, walking over and taking the iron from me. With the skill and grace of someone who knows what she's doing, she gets all the wrinkles out of my dark blue dress shirt.

"I need it for dinner tonight," I say, watching in awe as she does in two seconds what I've been failing to do for the last fifteen minutes.

"You have a date? I didn't know you were dating anyone."

"It's new," I say, feeling nerves flutter around in my stomach. "Her name is Maddie."

"Maddie? I don't think I know her." That's a very Mom-like thing to say, since she prides herself on knowing everyone in town.

"She just moved here. She lives in Shady Heights."

Boom. There it is. Mom's eyes widen and she suddenly seems to glow with appreciation and pride. "Shady Heights? Well, isn't that something."

I nod. "Her mom is engaged to Landon Howard. He lives near Mindy—"

Mom cuts me off. "I know exactly who he is. He's a great guy. Oh, this is so exciting!" Mom lifts my shirt off the ironing board and hands it to me, then proceeds to fold up the board herself and put it away. That's really saying something, because Mom is big on making us clean up after ourselves.

"Oh, honey, I am so proud of you. I want to meet this girl as soon as possible."

I roll my eyes. "Let's make sure she likes me first, okay?"

I already know she does like me, but Mom doesn't need to be privy to those details yet. The last thing I need during this glorious puppy love phase of my new relationship is for Maddie to meet my parents and have them ruin it. A Shady Heights girlfriend? Yeah, my parents will liken that to winning the lottery.

"Let me get you some money," Mom says, sauntering off into the kitchen.

"No, Mom, I'm fine," I call back, but it's useless.

She digs into her purse and pulls out three twenties. "Where are you going? Somewhere nice?"

"I have a reservation at William's Steakhouse," I say, knowing she'll approve.

She frowns and pulls out two more bills from her wallet. "This won't be enough, but it'll help. How much do you have?"

"Mom. I have *plenty* of money, I promise."

"William's is a nice place," she warns, shoving the cash in my hands. "You need to impress this girl. Get dessert, too. Order those fancy cocktail drinks without the alcohol."

I reach out and put my hands on Mom's shoulders, doing my best to peer down at her. Even though she's shorter than I am, she's still intimidating because she's my mom.

"I love you, Mom. But I've got this, okay? Trust me."

She heaves a sigh and then slowly smiles. "Okay, I'll trust you. You treat her well, okay? And have fun! You'll seem much more interesting if you're having fun."

Maddie meets me on the grand entrance steps to her massive house. They're painted shiny white and look cleaner than even the cleanest dishes in my own house.

"I would have knocked on the door," I say, as I get out of my car and walk over to her.

She's wearing a dark blue dress that matches my shirt, even though we didn't plan it, and black ballerina type shoes. Her bright pink hair is swept back and poufy on top, and I'm not sure how to describe it, but she looks cute as hell.

She sighs, and reaches for my hand so I can walk her to my car. "My mom was like freaking out about me having a date, so I didn't want you to come inside. She would have fawned over us like we were some freaking magical phenomenon or something, and it would have been embarrassing, so I just slipped out."

I can't help but chuckle. "My mom is the same way."

I open the door for her and she slides in, peering up at me with the cutest smile as I close the door and head over to my side of the car. "So, I hope you like fancy steakhouse food."

"Oh my God, I love steakhouses," she says, tossing her head back.

"Well, it's not like a Texas steakhouse . . . it's more sophisticated. They offer a ton of stuff, not just steak. They even have vegan food and stuff. It's pretty good."

"Cool," she says. Her hand slips over the console and wraps in mine. My knee is aching, but being near her makes the pain easy to ignore.

"Whoa," Maddie says as I drive up to the restaurant. It is a pretty awesome sight, the large building overlooking the river that runs through town. It's made of big slabs of rocks for bricks, and has a tree-lined entrance with all of the trees glowing with little clear lights. There are a ton of people here, like always, which is why I needed reservations. I pull up to the very front, and we get out so the valet can park the car.

"They actually have valets here?" Maddie says, her mouth open.

I wrap my arm around her waist and tug her close. "Of course. Why wouldn't they?"

She shrugs. "I thought that was like a Hollywood type thing. So fancy."

I find it a little weird that a girl who lives in Shady Heights has never used a valet, but I shrug it off. Maybe they take their own private jets to restaurants or something.

Maddie is in awe as we enter the restaurant, which looks more like an art museum than a place to eat. We're taken to our seats, where a candle glows on the table between us. The back wall is one large window that looks out at the river below. It's beautiful and dark in here, all ambiance and soft music playing from the live jazz band in the corner.

Maddie looks absolutely blown away, so I'm already feeling like a badass boyfriend right about now. I order one of the fancy drinks Mom had suggested, and Maddie agrees to try one with me.

Her brows pull together as she looks over the menu. I already know what I want: fried coconut shrimp with a baked potato and veggie skewer. At a place this fancy, they can even make the vegetables taste like heaven.

Maddie doesn't seem too impressed, though. "You okay?" I ask.

Her lips slide to the side of her mouth. "There are no prices on this menu."

That can't possibly be a new thing to her. Her future step-dad is freaking Landon Howard.

"It doesn't matter what it costs," I say, sipping from my drink. "Get whatever sounds good."

She bites on her lip. "That's the thing . . . I don't know what half of this food is." The moment she says it, she looks up at me, almost as if she's startled. She closes her eyes for a moment and takes a deep breath. "I just . . . we don't go out to eat very much and . . . I mean, I don't know. What should I get?"

"What do you like?"

She shrugs. "Everything, I guess."

"Are you allergic to anything?" I ask.

She shakes her head. I glance over the menu. "Well, everything they make is awesome. The steaks are good, but

I'm kind of obsessed with their coconut shrimp. Also the chicken is good. My mom loves the pasta, so you could try that . . ."

As I rattle off all of the delicious things to choose from, Maddie lowers her menu and watches me talk. There's something weird in her expression, but I'm not sure what. I don't think she's losing interest in me or anything like that. She just seems weird.

"What are you getting?" she asks after a while.

I tell her, and she nods. "I'll get that, too. If that's okay with you?"

I smile. "Of course it is."

Dinner goes well, but that little crease in Maddie's brow has me concerned. It almost feels like she's faking something, faking her happiness with me. It's killing me inside, but I don't want to be the guy who whines about the date, so I try to play it cool.

"Would you like to take a walk down to the river?" I ask her as we're leaving the restaurant. "They have a little viewing area down there."

"Okay," she says. When she takes my hand, it feels as if some of her desire to be close to me has faded away.

Alarm bells go off in my head, and I try to recount the entire date, everything I said and did and all the times we laughed. Did I do something wrong?

We walk down to the pier, but it's kind of a stupid idea because there's a few other people out here, ruining the privacy. There's even an older couple making out on a nearby bench, their hands and mouths going places no decent person would approve of in public.

We walk to the end of the pier and I let go of her hand, turning to face her. "Are you okay? Something seems off."

"I'm fine," she says in that high-pitched voice that tells me she's lying.

I frown. William's is hands down, the best restaurant within an hour of Louetta, so I know it was the best place to take her on our first real date. I've been a gentleman and I've tried being funny and likable, so why does she seem so very unamused?

"Maddie, you seem weird. Did I do something?"

She peers up at me, that look in her eyes exactly the same as when we're in the middle of making out. That's good, I guess. I reach for her hands. "You can tell me."

Her shoulders lift as she takes a deep breath. "Okay, well I guess I feel weird. I don't know."

She looks at the ground and I squeeze her hands. "Why do you feel weird? Up until tonight, it seemed like we were both equally crazy about each other."

Her lips press together and then she looks back up at me. "I do like you. A lot. I guess I'm just not used to fancy stuff like this." She nods back toward the restaurant. "It's a little much . . ."

My eyebrows pull together. "You didn't like it?"

She shakes her head. "No, I did. It was nice, but it was kind of . . . *too* nice?" The look on her face tells me how guilty she feels admitting this all to me, and I try my best not to get offended. My heart is thudding like crazy and all I want is to make her happy. It's a crap feeling knowing my best efforts have failed.

"I'm sorry, Maddie." I run my hand down her cheek, then tilt her forehead up to my lips. "I just wanted to impress you."

"I know, and that's sweet of you. But seriously, I'd be happy with a pizza and a movie at home, or something."

I grin. "You're an M, now, Maddie. Didn't Mindy tell you you're supposed to be wined and dined?"

She rolls her eyes. "I know I live in Shady Heights, but I'm just not used to all of this fancy stuff. I come from . . . well, *not* Shady Heights. And when I'm in a place like this restaurant, I just feel like everyone *knows*. Like all these fancy people take one look at me and know I don't belong."

"That's not true," I say, sliding my hands around her waist. "All these people are either jealous that you're the most beautiful girl in the room, or they're too busy hating me for getting to date the prettiest girl in the room."

She grins sheepishly and looks down, then moves forward and presses her cheek to my chest. I feel her arms slide around my back, holding me closely. "Thank you," she murmurs against my shirt. "For dinner, and everything."

"I should be thanking you," I say, letting my chin rest on top of her head. "You make me the luckiest guy on earth."

27

MADDIE

BEFORE LONG, my old life is like a horrible nightmare that I've somehow managed to escape. As weeks go by, Colby and I become the picture perfect teenage couple, and Mindy slowly becomes my favorite person and best friend. She's really not as bitchy as she seems, once you get to know her. At school, she's a little . . . much, at times, but when it's just us hanging out at one of our houses, she's a normal person. It's really nice having a best friend, now.

Almost as nice as having a boyfriend like Colby. He's sweet, and attentive, and kind. He's a great kisser. Though our makeouts are getting more intense each day, he hasn't pushed me into going farther than I want to. In short: my life is perfect.

That doesn't stop me from waking up in a cold sweat in the middle of the night, nightmares of my old life haunting me. I used to eat instant noodles and stale bread. Now I eat whatever the hell I want, cooked fresh by our own personal chef. I used to wear my one bra every day, even after safety-pinning it together when the hooks broke. Now, Mom takes me shopping so often that I can't even remember where I bought each of the bras in my closet. My sisters are benefiting the most, because now their life is full of fun times with Mom, trips to museums and the movies, and all the food they could ever want.

My new life is a surreal, crazy change from my old one. I wish I could live happily in it, only caring about the present.

But the bitter truth is that part of this new life is a total lie. Every time Mindy or Colby says something about my old life, I have to lie, mumble, or change the subject.

At least once a day at school, I get all nervous and shaky when the teacher talks to me, scared they'll reveal that I'm not really a new girl at all. Luckily, it's not like anyone *told* my teachers I'm new. They all just realized one of their students dyed their hair. They don't talk to me and I don't talk to them. But it's still scary.

I had to avoid Jacoby like the plague for a week, but then he got arrested for dealing drugs on school property and now he's in alternative school. Score one for the Universe looking out for me.

On Monday after school, Mindy comes over a few minutes after Colby drops me off. Lately he's been taking me to get a coffee or ice cream or something after school, that way we have more time together, but today he has to help his dad clean out the garage so he leaves early.

It's a shame because even five minutes away from Colby makes my heart hurt.

"So, I take it things with lover boy are still good?" Mindy says, plopping down on my bed.

Pam is in here vacuuming the floor, so she finishes quickly and asks if we want anything to drink. I tell her no, before Mindy can answer. It's my goal to make Pam work as little as possible because I get really weirded out by having a servant in the house.

"Yep, things are perfect," I say, my voice all dreamy as I fall onto the bed next to Mindy.

"I never would have imagined that you'd fall so hard and so fast for Colby Jensen, of all people," she says. She looks over at me, her black and blue hair falling into her eyes. "But I'm happy for you anyway."

"Thanks," I say. It's really awesome to have a best friend, even though I know Maria is still annoyed by it. "What's Matilda up to?" I ask, while we both lay on our stomachs across my bed, feet dangling off the end, focus on our cell phones.

"Banging her boyfriend, I guess," Mindy says with a snort. "That guy is pretty hot for a senior. You'll learn that about us as time goes on, Maddie. I'm the logical one who is holding out for a *real* man, Matilda dates a new guy every month and is like, totally MIA when she's in a new relationship, and Maria goes from being your best friend to your worst enemy every other day or so."

"Really?" I ask, while I scroll through Instagram. "So she's not just hating me to hate me?"

Mindy shakes her head. "Nah. She'll come around and hang out with us soon. It's a little different though, because the three of us have been best friends for years. We don't just add a new M all the time or anything."

"Well, I'm glad you added me," I say, tapping the heart on

every photo I scroll through. "Otherwise I'd be some friendless loser in school."

She scoffs. "No way. Everyone loves you. If I didn't snag you, some other bitch would have, and then I'd have to hate you on principle." She scoots over until our shoulders are touching, and readies the camera on her phone. "Smile!"

I lean my head next to hers and we take an adorable selfie, which she posts online.

"I'm so glad you moved here," Mindy says.

"Yeah," I say, feeling that boulder of guilt settle in the pit of my stomach. "Me too."

I wonder what she'd do if she knew I'd been here all along? She likes me now that I'm a Shady Heights resident, but I'm still the same person I was when I lived in a trailer park. Yet, the Mindy Carmichaels of the world aren't friends with trailer park girls.

That's why, no matter how close we get, I can't ever tell her the truth.

28

COLBY

I AM in love with Maddie Sinclair.

Forget everything I ever thought I knew, all the other girls I dated and liked a lot. All of that is total crap because my one true love is Maddie. Even Josh's mom was wrong on this one. True love *can* be found in high school. When I am with Maddie, there's nothing in the world that can get me down.

I haven't told her, not yet. Haven't looked deep into her eyes and said the words, "I love you."

Maddie is a logical, practical, smart girl. She probably wouldn't be too excited to hear those epic words so soon in our relationship. It's only been about a month, and I still haven't met her parents. She's met mine, several times. They love her, as I knew they would.

Since Maddie is busy helping her mom plan her wedding, she doesn't want to complicate things by introducing them to me just yet. I can understand that. I'm also excited to meet her sisters because they are such a huge part of her life. We're taking things slow here, so I can't tell her I love her just yet.

But, dammit, I love her.

Now that my parents know how serious my dating life is, I'd hoped I could use it as another argument for getting a job. I prepared my argument and brought it up on a good day when they were in good moods. I said I'd like to take my girl-friend out on dates every week and I'd like to pay for it myself. I humbled myself by saying I'd prefer to pay for my dates with money I earned, not money they earned.

They didn't fall for it. Mom asked if Mindy has to work and I'd said no, even though I wanted to lie and say yes to help my cause. My parents then decided that if a Shady Heights girl didn't need a job, then neither did I. Dad said he was fine pitching in money for my dates.

How awkward is that? After all my careful planning, I'm still screwed on the job front.

I shove all of those thoughts aside as I shower and go over my whole body twice with the soap. Tonight is date night with the prettiest girl on the planet, and I can't let my parents' stupid decisions put a damper on that.

After our first date, I learned to include Maddie on our date night planning. She's not too big on fancy restaurants, which is weird for a normal girl in our school, but uniquely normal for Maddie. She's not high maintenance, not stuck up, not demanding of me like every other girl in my life has been at one time or another.

She loves going to the Burger Shack for burgers and fries, or James Coney Island for a hot dog and milkshake. She's happy when we take a walk through the outlet mall, or see a movie at the theater with loveseats so we can cuddle.

In short, she's the perfect girlfriend ever. I throw on a pair of jeans and Maddie's favorite shirt, a black T-shirt with a blue surf shop logo on it.

I'm pulling on my shoes when Maddie calls me.

"Hey, beautiful," I say, wedging the phone between my ear and shoulder.

"Do you mind if I drive over to your house a little early?" she asks, sounding like she's already in the car.

"Sure. Is something wrong?"

"No, they're just doing wedding set up stuff and a million people are at our house and it's annoying. I wanted to get out of there, so I thought I could just come over if that's okay with you."

"Of course," I say, tying my shoe.

"Good, because I'm here."

Grinning, I jog through my house and fling open the front door, forgetting that I'm still on the phone with her. She cuts the engine and gets out of her car, looking gorgeous as always. She's wearing these shorts with frilly stuff on the edges so they kind of look like a skirt, and a tank top that shows of her newly acquired tan. All those days at the pool have turned her golden like caramel.

"Hey, babe," I say, rushing forward and wrapping my arms around her.

I kiss her, the feeling electric now that I know for sure that I love her. She smells like lavender and cotton candy, and it fills me with all kinds of fluttery feelings that Josh would rag on me for having.

I slide my hands down her soft arms and then grab her waist and pull her to me, kissing her even as she giggles at me.

"Are we going out or are we just gonna stand here kissing all night?" she says, poking me in the chest.

"Hmmm, both ideas sound good," I say, pressing her back against her car as I keep kissing her, taking in the glorious way her lips feel against mine.

She sighs a little, sliding her fingers up my chest. Goosebumps cover my skin, her touch like a flame that I can't ever get enough of.

"I guess we should go out," she says with a little pained sigh. "I mean, I am kinda hungry and although I love making out with you, you don't fill my stomach."

I laugh, and kiss her one last time. "Okay. Let me get my keys and we'll go."

"You want to take my car?" she asks, holding out the car keys on her index finger.

I consider it a moment. My car is probably faster, but hers smells like new car while mine smells like, well, like a locker room.

"Sounds like a plan," I say, taking the keys.

***

After dinner, we end up at the community park where they're showing the movie Jaws on a huge inflatable screen. The movie is at the bottom of a wide sloping grassy hill, and people spread out everywhere on towels and blankets to watch it.

There's not much of a crowd here tonight, so Maddie and

I find a secluded spot in front of a tree at the very back row. From here, we can chat and make out without bothering anyone.

"Have I ever told you how lucky I am?" I ask. Maddie is laying on her back on top of the blanket she had in her car from the last time we were here. My hoodie, also left in her car, is being used as her pillow, and I'm on my side, my head propped up on my elbow right next to her.

She shakes her head. "I'm the lucky one."

I purse my lips together. "Nope. It's me. And I'll argue all night with you to prove I'm right."

A slow grin slides across her lips, and she reaches up, wrapping her fingers around my neck and pulling me down to her level. She kisses me deeply, her tongue roaming across mine, the fireworks between us bursting at full volume. I grab her thigh and pull her against me, moving to kiss her neck, her collarbone, the little curve of flesh just above her shirt's neckline.

She moans as I rock against her, my hands sliding all over her sexy as hell curves. She grabs my back, her nails digging into my skin, pulling me all the way on top of her.

This goes on for longer than it should in a public place, no matter how secluded we are. I pull away slowly, letting my hand cup her face while I kiss her one last time. "We should stop," I whisper, both to maintain public decency, and because I might literally explode if this goes any further. I'm trying to be a gentleman here.

"See?" Maddie says, grinning and looking a little woozy from all of our making out. "I'm the lucky one."

"Why do you say that?" I ask, gazing into her eyes.

She shrugs, reality coming back to her features. "Trust me. My life wasn't that great before my mom got engaged to Landon."

"Really?" I ask, brushing the hair out of her eyes. "You can tell me more, if you'd like."

She shakes her head. "I can't. You probably wouldn't like me if I did."

I lift an eyebrow. "Why would you say that? I'm crazy about you."

"Well, I guess, I just wasn't popular or anything at my old school."

"So? I don't like you because you're popular, you dork," I say, placing a quick kiss on top of her nose. "I like you because of *you*."

She shakes her head slightly. "You wouldn't have ever noticed me if Mindy didn't, like, make me one of her popular friends."

"Wrong!" I say. "I noticed you at Mrs. Ruiz' house, remember? It was before you knew Mindy." I stick out my tongue. "So there. I win."

She makes this little laugh and then gazes out at the sky. "Let's just be happy with how things are and not question the past."

It's a little after midnight when we part ways after an amazing date. I'm crawling into bed when my phone goes off and I check it, expecting something from Maddie.

Maria's name appears at the top of the text. Ugh.

I ignore her message asking to hang out. I ignore it when she says it's important, and I ignore the dirty picture message she sends afterward. I even ignore it when she says she's better than Maddie, but that time, it's a little harder to hold my tongue.

29

MADDIE

I STARE LONGINGLY at the text on my cell phone. It's simple and cute, an *I miss you* with a crying face emoji. I only left his house ten minutes ago, so he can't possibly miss me, yet he does. And I miss him, his touch more than anything.

I never imagined feeling this way about a guy back in my old life. I always thought trying to date while worrying about how the bills will get paid or who will babysit the girls because Mom's working late would make it impossible. Now all of those problems are gone and I'm free to live the life of a carefree teenager.

Mom and Landon's wedding is in a week, next Friday. They've invited Landon's parents and family, my aunt Cindy who lives in Louisiana and her husband, and a couple friends. Mom and Landon have asked me to invite Colby if I want to, but I haven't yet. I'm not sure if I want to invite him to something so intimate and close to my family.

I haven't even let him meet my parents yet. Mr. and Mrs. Jensen are super nice people and they seem to really like me, so meeting his parents wasn't as bad as I'd imagined. Maybe letting Mom and Landon meet Colby also won't be bad, but I'm not ready to find out.

I'm just so nervous about it. My new life with Landon as a future step-dad is one impossibly amazing, surreal life. I have a hard enough time getting used to living in this luxurious mansion with my mom and sisters.

My school life, the one I share with Colby, is another insanely impossible bliss that I wouldn't trade for anything. But right now, the home life and school life are two separate things.

There's been so much change in my life, it's hard dealing with it all. I still wake up in a panic attack from nightmares about being thrown back into the trailer park without a dime to our name. If Colby ever found out about that part of my life, I don't know what I'd do.

I'd probably just drop dead from mortification.

So, I heave a heavy sigh and look at the pale yellow Post-it note with Colby's name on it. I'm working on the seating chart for the wedding, and I keep putting him in the chair next to me and then taking him back off.

Mom and Landon really want to meet him and hope he comes to the wedding. I'm just not sure the perfect time to introduce my new boyfriend to my mom is on the day she's getting married.

I gnaw on my bottom lip and put the Post-it note back on the seating chart. In all, there's twenty relatives and friends attending, plus my sisters, me and Landon and Mom. Twenty-five people, total. That's a nice number. Adding Colby would just mess it all up, right?

As much as I try to justify my brain's choice to exclude Colby, my heart doesn't really listen. I like Colby. A lot. I might even love him. That means he shouldn't be pushed away.

But the idea of merging my new home life with my new school life is downright terrifying. Like, what if Emma says something about our old house or about how we've lived here in town longer than just a few weeks?

My stomach twists at the idea. I pull off the Post-it note, crumple it in my hand and toss it on the floor. It's settled then. No Colby at the wedding.

Colby won't be welcomed inside my house at all until it's been long enough that neither my sisters or my mom will mention how long we've really lived here.

On the Monday before Mom's wedding, I'm barely paying attention to the stories at our lunch table. Although my wedding planning binder is at home, I'm still going over the plans in my head. We've ordered the food, the flowers, the table settings.

Emma and Starla have matching adorable flower girl dresses, and Mindy helped me buy a lavender dress that looks incredible. She was cool with not being invited to the wedding, especially after I told her it was family only, a small ceremony in our backyard. I get the feeling Mindy is the kind of girl who prefers to party big.

We've ordered round tables to set up under the patio, and a dance floor is being installed for the night. The pool will have floating candles to give it all a romantic glow. Even for a small wedding, it'll be glamorous and wonderful.

The closer we get to the actual day, the happier I feel, for Mom, for my sisters, and for me. Our new life really is here to stay. I finish eating my salad and rise from the table to throw away my trash. When I'm walking back, my eyes catch Colby's, and even though I was just sitting next to him not five seconds ago, he gives me this devilish look that melts my insides.

I'm about to sit down next to him again when he grabs my waist and pulls me into his lap. I wrap my arms around his shoulders, peering up at him.

"We're not supposed to sit like this in the cafeteria," I say, pretending to scold him.

He shrugs. "I don't care."

We kiss, and Mindy makes a gagging sound from the next seat over.

"Oh, good. There you are."

We both glance up to find Maria walking toward us, an expensive school camera slung around her neck.

"About time you showed up for lunch," Mindy says, stabbing into a piece of lettuce with a little more force than necessary. Now that she mentions it, there has been a nice lack of Maria and her evil glares for the past few days.

Maria gives Mindy a tight-lipped smile. "Yearbook," she says by way of explanation. She hefts a black and gold hardback book onto the table, directly in front of me. When her eyes meet mine, they sparkle with an excitement I haven't before seen on her. "It's so weird how you only just started school," she says, my blood turning cold beneath her glare.

She reaches for the book, the yearbook, and opens it to a bookmarked page. My heart seems to stop as her manicured nail slides down the silky paper, stopping at a picture of me, taken back in January.

"Picture day was months ago," she says, using this fake childlike voice. "*So* weird that your photo is in here."

"What the hell?" Mindy says, leaning on her elbows to get a better look.

Behind me, Colby's chest tightens as he is without a doubt staring at the same thing. Me, with brown stringy hair, a worn out shirt, and no makeup except for my dollar store clumpy mascara.

I don't have to look over to the left to know that the name *Maddie Sinclair* is printed there, black and white proof that I did not move here during Spring Break. I am a fraud. And now everyone knows it.

I push off Colby's lap, grab my backpack from the floor, and run.

30

COLBY

MINDY STANDS UP, her hands slapping the table hard as she levels a glare at Maria. "What the hell is your problem?" she hisses.

It's more than I do. I just sit here, staring at a color photo of Maddie, my girlfriend, looking not at all like she looks now. Her hair is different, sure, but everything else is, too. She seems far away, distant. Maybe even lost. The girl in the photo is a girl who has given up on life.

Why is she in the yearbook? Picture day was months ago.

Mindy slaps me on the shoulder, jarring me from staring at the yearbook. "Well?" she says, giving me this look that very much resembles when my mother is pissed at me.

"Well, what?" I say, finally able to find my voice.

Mindy throws a hand behind her. "Are you going to go get her?"

I glance back, but Maddie is gone. There's a knot in my stomach that's growing bigger with each second. This is confusing as hell, but there has to be an explanation. There is an answer to why Maddie's picture is here in the yearbook. But the fact that she just ran away like that, without even telling me the answer, makes me pause.

I shake my head. "Why would I go after someone who ran away from me?"

Mindy's jaw hardens. "Because you're her boyfriend, you jerk."

She lets out a huff and turns to go after Maddie herself, but Maria stops her.

"I know the truth, if you want to hear it. I'm not so sure your new best friend will tell it to you." Maria smirks. "But I will."

"What the hell could you possibly know?" I ask, wondering if this is all some evil plot that she's concocted in her efforts to make me want her.

Maria takes her time sitting across from us at the table. She leans forward a little, no doubt purposely pushing her boobs up and out. How she doesn't get pulled for dress code with that much cleavage showing, I don't know.

"I noticed this picture the other day, and I thought the same thing. I mean, she just moved here, so she wouldn't be in the yearbook. Then, I paid a visit to her house and talked with the maid." She pauses, probably for dramatic effect because she looks right at me, expecting me to react. I don't.

The maid told me that Maddie and her mom lived here for months, and only just moved into Landon Howard's house in Shady Heights a month ago during Spring Break. Maddie dyed her hair right after she moved in and decided to pretend to be someone else. Even her homeroom teacher confirms it. Mrs. Brooks said Maddie used to wear the same outfits every day and then suddenly she became this pink-haired Louis Vuitton carrying popular princess."

"Shut your bitch mouth," Mindy says, her fangs coming out in full force. "You're never happy until you're destroying everyone else."

"Right, because I'm the one who lied to you for the last month?" she says, her thick eyeliner narrowing at Mindy.

They keep at it, bitching back and forth, but it's all white noise to me. I remember a time not too long ago when Maddie confided in me that she's not sure Mindy really cares about her as a friend, or if it's all just some popular girl thing to piss off her other friends. Well, I know now that Mindy does care. She's fighting like hell to protect Maddie's honor since she's not here to defend herself.

But that's just it. She's not here. She ran away before explaining herself. That means she has something to hide, and she's hiding it from me.

I stare at the picture again, at the girl who is so devoid of life compared to the girl I know now as Maddie Sinclair. My fingers go tingly as panic rises up my spine. I have fallen in love with a girl I don't even know.

What happened to her to make her this way?

And why did she lie about it?

31

———

MADDIE

THE ROAD BLURS as I drive home, my eyes filling with tears faster than I can wipe them away. A dark voice in my sub-conscious laughs at me. I knew this would happen, after all. Didn't I? People don't get to pretend to be someone else forever. Eventually you get caught.

Eventually you lose everything.

I slam the button on my gate opener and the metal slowly moves inward, letting me drive into this massive driveway that I don't deserve. Landon's car is in the garage, which is a little weird since he normally works until five every day. He probably took off early today to keep working on wedding stuff with Mom. Great. Just what I need: a whole family to see me crying my eyes out.

I park, climb out, and go straight to my room without running into anyone.

My chest is on fire with how painful this feels. I fall face first on my bed, tuck my arms under the pillow, and cry. It doesn't help the pain, and it doesn't make me feel better, but I keep crying anyway.

My phone never rings; the doorbell never chimes. No one comes to check on me. Not Mindy, not Colby.

Colby, the world's best boyfriend. From the moment we met, I knew I didn't deserve him, but I lied to myself and said I did. Now he knows the truth. His resulting silence speaks volumes. I don't know how much time passes while I lay here crying into my pillow. The fabric is soaked, my eyes are swollen, and the ache in my chest feels like a Mac truck slammed into me.

Several hours later, I hear my sisters yelling excitedly about something downstairs. Mom's voice follows soon after, something like "Maddie's car is here!"

There's a soft knock on my door and then it opens. I don't look over; I just keep my head buried in my pillow.

"Maddie?" Mom says. "Are you okay? When did you get home?"

"I'd like to be alone, please."

She's quiet for a moment, and I turn to see if she left and just didn't shut the door. But she's still there, a little line creasing down her forehead.

"Honey!" she says, rushing into my room. "You're crying! What happened?"

I shake my head, turn around and hide in the soaking wet pillow. I wish I could tap my heels together three times and disappear. Starla says something from the hallway, and Mom asks Emma to take her down to the living room. "We'll just be a minute," she tells her.

Mom's hand touches my back. "Maddie, tell me what's wrong."

I take in a shaking breath and then roll over to face her. Mom and I have been through so many things together. I've always been her rock when she needed me, and she's always been mine. But I've never screwed up this badly.

She gives me this small smile, probably hoping it'll coax me out of being silent. Her hand brushes hair from my face, and I notice the sparkle from her engagement ring. Her wedding is in a few days. I can't unload all of this drama on her now. She doesn't need it.

"I'm fine, Mom."

Her eyes narrow. "I'm not an idiot, Maddie. Is it boy trouble? Did you and Colby fight?"

I look away, tears forming in my eyes again. Mom makes this comforting sound as she runs her fingers through my hair like she used to do when I was younger and had the flu.

"It's worse than that," I murmur, looking at my fingers. "I lied to him. I lied to everyone."

Mom quirks an eyebrow. "How'd you do that?"

I decide to tell her everything. Maybe she'll have something comforting to say, some way to console me after this nightmare. Or maybe she'll be so pissed she'll disown me. Whatever the case, I take a deep breath and tell her the biggest lie of my life.

Two days pass. I don't go to school out of total mortification, even though my mother thinks I should just face the hell that

I've brought onto myself. She wasn't too pissed at me, but she did yell at Landon for encouraging me to go along with the lie. That part freaked me out a lot. They're about to get married, and we're about to get to live here happy and safe and taken care of for as long as that lasts. When she yelled at him, I feared it would all fall apart and we'd be kicked out.

Landon didn't react like I thought he would. He apologized to her, and to me, He said he should have thought it through more before he encouraged me to do something stupid. And then Mom and Landon made up and we all had a great dinner together with Pam and my sisters. If I hadn't already known for sure that Landon is better than any other man in Mom's past, now I know.

I'm faking like everything is slowly getting better, but I know I'll have to go back to school soon enough. I can't, though. I just can't.

Colby has ignored me for two entire days. He hasn't sent a single text, or called, or even posted anything to social media. I've been too scared to talk to him, too afraid of what mean thing he might reply. I guess it's safe to say we're broken up now, and the very thought sends me into a darkness so painful I don't ever want to get out of bed.

I had everything I could ever want, and I ruined it.

Colby doesn't want me, not anymore. He wanted the girl he thought I was. By now, surely they all know I was the trailer trash loser who lived in the pedophile house. I might still live in a house in Shady Heights, but I am no longer a member of this world.

I'll dye my hair back brown, I'll trade in my new clothes for simple ones, and I'll go back to school and pretend it never happened. Maybe that way the M's and the football players and Colby himself will be able to forget about me.

Maybe it'll be easier this way.

The doorbell chimes around four o'clock on Wednesday. It's probably a delivery of more wedding stuff. We've had packages arrive daily for a week now.

I'm lying in my bed, still wearing the pajamas I slept in, my hair a messy pile on top of my head. The only way I could think of to remove all traces of my old life was to do a factory reset on my phone, after deleting Instagram of course. Now, instead of Colby and me smiling at the camera as my wallpaper, I have a default image of a sunflower.

Too bad my brain still remembers the way it used to be. If only I could do a factory reset on my memories.

My door pushes open without warning, a sure sign that Emma or Starla are wandering in to play with me.

"Not now, kiddo," I say over my shoulder as I heave a sigh.

"I'm not a kid."

Mindy's voice freezes me in place. "Why are you here?" I say, not looking back.

She walks around my bed, her perfume fruity and strong. She's holding a backpack, which she heaves onto my bed and unzips, revealing a six pack of beer. She takes one, cracks the top and hands it to me.

I sit up in bed, gazing at the cold beer in my hand. I lift an eyebrow, but Mindy just stares at me for a beat.

She says, "Tell me everything."

32

COLBY

YOU KNOW THAT SAYING, *it's too good to be true?* That's exactly what dating Maddie was like. She was beautiful, smart, funny. She was also an M. A Shady Heights girl.

The simple fact that a Shady Heights girl both: A) wanted to date me, and B) didn't expect me to spend tons of money on her, was too good to be true.

Yet I was the dumbass who went and believed it.

So I guess my broken heart is just a product of my own fault. I should have known better. True love doesn't happen in high school.

True love doesn't happen for me.

In the days that follow, Mindy distances herself, choosing to eat lunch alone, or with someone else. I don't know. All I know is she isn't currently talking to Maria, who has taken the opportunity to dive straight back into my life, flirting endlessly as if her own life depended on it.

I ignore her for two days straight, simply choosing to focus my attention on Bryce and Josh and pretend she wasn't sitting next to me. By the third day, when she walks into the cafeteria with her Diet Coke and basket of powdered donuts that she eats for lunch, I push my backpack onto the seat next to me.

She lifts an eyebrow. "Uh, excuse you?"

"Excuse you," I say, keeping my hand protectively on my backpack. "This seat is reserved for my girlfriend."

Maria narrows her eyes. "It doesn't seem like you have a girlfriend right now, plus I've been sitting here for two days."

"It's always a great day to find a new place to sit. So why don't you try it out?" I reply with equal venom. Her nostrils flare, but she doesn't say anything else before turning on her heel and stomping away.

"Dude," Bryce says, shaking his head as he takes another bite of his pizza. I guess that's all he plans on saying because all of his attention goes back to his food.

Josh's eyes flit over to me. "You talk to her yet?"

I shake my head. Stare at my food.

"You probably should."

I know he's right. But I don't say anything. I'm too hurt, pissed off, betrayed—hell, I don't even know what I am. Just that I'm not okay. After Maria's dramatic little exposé on my girlfriend, the whole truth of Maddie's existence came out like a tidal wave of betrayal.

She'd been a student here for months. She lied about it all when she moved to Shady Heights.

Those are the facts.

The question I still don't have answered though, is why?

Was this some made-for-TV movie scheme where someone bet her she couldn't infiltrate the M's and make a football player fall in love with her? Is she off laughing about it somewhere with her real friends? Was I the butt of some awful joke?

This thought cuts me to the core. I'd given my heart to this girl, meant every single thing I ever told her. And her contribution to our relationship? It was all a lie.

How could I have been so stupid?

After lunch, Josh finds me on my way to athletics, even though he's almost always late to class.

"Hey man," he says, falling into step with me.

The tone of his voice tells me there's more he has to say, so I just look over and wait for him to say it.

"You need to talk to her," he says, his normally happy-go-lucky expression now serious. "You can't just give up on her. Hear her out."

"She hasn't called me," I say, staring at the tiles on the floor. I've checked my phone more times than I care to admit.

"So call her."

A moment of silence passes and Josh clears his throat. "Look, I'm no expert or anything, but you can't just go on ignoring each other. I know you really liked this girl and Maria ambushed her, so it wasn't even a fair fight. Just talk to her and see what she says. Maybe you can get closure or something."

Coach stands in the doorway of the locker room, looking right at us, so I'm not about to say anything too revealing when a teacher is around. I look over at Josh, and I lie to him. "Yeah, maybe I'll do that."

33

______

MADDIE

MY REFLECTION LOOKS BACK at me. It's clearly disappointed. It's wondering how I can be wearing such a beautiful dress and still look like a horrible person. Maybe because this is just a normal dress, not some magical bad-decision-erasing dress from a mysterious and far away land.

Nope, I am in the real world. And I'm a terrible person.

In one hour, my mom will marry Landon and this will be the happiest day of her life. So I stare at my reflection in the tall mirror in my room and tell it to smile, stand tall, and look happy. So what if it's all for show?

This is Mom's night, not mine. I have the rest of my life to wallow in the self-pity of having ruined my shot at love with the greatest guy ever.

Mindy thinks I should talk to him. After a very painful talk that lasted for three hours, where I told her absolutely everything, she decided to forgive me. I told her about that day I tried applying for a job at the ice cream shop and she was there with the other M's and didn't even see me. I told her about how I feel when Colby enters a room, and how great it felt to have a boy care about me for the first time. After revealing every lie and every cover up—I even told her about the date with Jacoby—she'd agreed that she might have done the same thing in my position. Then she made fun of me, saying she should have known I wasn't raised with money by the way I acted. I think that's what makes her like me. Underneath it all, I'm just a normal person.

The good news is that Mindy still wants to be friends. The bad news is that Colby still hasn't called me. Mindy thinks I should just give him time. I think I should give him the entire planet while I move away to Mars and never come back again.

Pam comes in the room, my sisters holding each of her hands. They're both dressed like tiny little flower girls, their hair all curled and styled with a tiara.

I lean forward and put my hands on my knees. "Girls! You both look so pretty!"

They grin, and Emma shows me her basket of white rose petals. "We get to throw them on the ground and we don't even have to pick them up," she says, grinning mischievously like the idea of leaving a mess on the floor is getting away with something truly evil.

"That's just one of the reasons weddings are fun," I say. "Are we ready to go downstairs?"

In the backyard, the guests mingle and drink wine. I've already met all of Landon's family members over the previous days, and my Aunt is too busy chowing down on appetizers to bother trying to talk to me, which is a good thing because I'm not in the mood for small talk.

I leave the girls with Pam and then head inside to find my mom in her dressing room, which is really just one of the spare guest rooms. The makeup artist and hair stylist are working hard on her, transforming her into a princess for this special night.

"Honey," Mom says, looking at me through the mirror in front of her because she can't turn her head while it's being styled. "You look beautiful."

"Not as beautiful as you," I say, sitting on an ottoman near her feet. "Are you excited?"

Mom grins. "Very."

When the stylists are finally done, I walk with Mom down to where the wedding guests are all waiting to see her. We stop just inside the double doors that lead to the backyard where Mom will make her entrance. Well, we *both* will. She's asked me to walk her down the aisle.

My sisters ooh and ahh over Mom's pretty dress, and Mom kisses them both on the tops of their heads.

"Thirty seconds and the flower girls will go out," our wedding planner says. She's a tall thin woman with her hair always pulled back in a severe bun. She winks at my mom as she walks past.

I hold out my elbow, and Mom loops her arm into mine. The doors open and my sisters step out, reveling in the attention and the beauty of the night. Our backyard has been transformed into an outdoor ballroom, the pool sparkling like a chandelier.

"I take it you didn't invite Colby?"

Hearing his name sends a stab of pain through my heart. I shake my head.

Mom frowns. "Well, I hope you two find a way to work things out."

"I don't think that'll happen," I say, staring at the doors in front of us. In the distance, wedding music plays, and all of our family is out there waiting on Mom and Landon to tie the knot. Talking about Colby is the last thing on my mind right now.

"Honey," Mom says as the wedding planner ushers us forward to make our debut on the makeshift wedding aisle. "I am living proof that real love will find you someday, even if you don't think it ever will. If what you had with Colby was real, don't fret. He'll find his way back to you."

I give her a sad smile and the doors open. Everyone turns to look at us, and they even stand from their chairs. "Thanks, Mom," I say as we step forward. "I love you."

She squeezes my hand as she prepares to become a wife. "I love you, too, honey."

34

———

COLBY

I BLOW off my friends on Friday. They're going to the Getaway with the sole purpose of picking up girls, and that couldn't be more unappealing to me right now.

My parents don't ask why I'm staying in tonight. I haven't told them about Maddie, but it'd be obvious even to the most absent of parents. When it comes to breakups, my parents prefer to leave me alone and let me work it out myself. I guess that's better than having some heartfelt family meeting over it.

Mindy calls me around seven, and I let it go to voicemail. She's been nearly as MIA as Maddie lately, eating lunch alone and going dark on social media. At least she didn't delete her account like Maddie did. Of course, I can't ever picture Mindy doing something like that. She lives for the attention of internet likes.

A few seconds after the ringing stops, it starts again. With a sigh, I answer Mindy's second call.

"Yeah?"

"Douche bag," she says by way of greeting. "I'm coming over."

"No, you're not, Mindy. I don't need company."

"I'm here. Come let me in."

"No," I say, standing up and peering out of my window. "Go home."

"Not happening, Jensen."

I know she won't give up; that's just not the Mindy way. I hang up on her and walk to the front door, where she meets me on the doorstep, staring at her nails like she's bored.

"You gonna invite me in?" she says.

I step back and open the door wider. "Don't bother asking for a drink because you won't be here long."

She makes this little scoffing sound and moves around me, heading toward my room. Luckily my parents aren't here or they'd stop her and chat because she's another Shady Heights girl and my parents are all about having friends in high places.

In my room, I close the door, turn around and fold my arms across my chest. "Why are you here?"

She sits on the edge of my bed, facing the window. "We need to talk about Maddie."

"Did she send you here?" I ask, sitting next to her. Just hearing her name makes my heart pound.

"She did not. But I came here because you two are both my friends and I care about you."

"Caring about us doesn't make everything all right, Carmichael."

Mindy throws her hair over her shoulder and turns to

look at me. Most guys cower under her calculated gaze, but I don't. I've known her too long.

"I had a talk with our girl yesterday. Now that I learned the truth about her, I decided to forgive her for lying to me."

Okay, that's not at all what I'd expected her to say. My shoulders loosen a little. "You're not really the forgiving type," I say.

Mindy shrugs. "I understood where she was coming from. I think maybe that's why I like Maddie so much—she's real. She got that way by living a really hard life, and now she's living the high life with us but she's still grounded as a person. I can respect that."

The cracks in my broken heart feel like they're breaking apart all over again. "Yeah, but she lied to us. To me. I loved her and she lied to me."

"I don't blame her one bit. Look at you! You never noticed her before she was rich." She turns to look at me, a surprising lack of sarcasm on her face. "Listen up, Jensen. I'm going to tell you everything I know, and you're going to pay very close attention. Then I'm leaving, and you can do what you want with the information. If you ruin this then that's your own fault, but I'm doing my part, okay? So listen well."

I take a deep breath. My body feels weird in this suit. A little sweaty even though I just showered. Itchy even though the fabric is soft. I guess it's my nerves.

Maddie Sinclair is the perfect girl for me, and she's been

here the whole time. My angel, my perfect girl, was hiding in plain sight.

I never even saw her before. I had four months to discover this girl and make her mine, but I only saw what I wanted to see. The popular crowd. I failed her and I failed myself.

So now I'm going to a wedding in the best suit I own.

I take a deep breath and run the comb through my hair, tugging it into place at the back of my neck. My stomach is so jumbled up with nerves that I may never eat again, and I'm sweating through three layers of deodorant.

I draw in a deep breath and head down to my car, driving straight to Maddie's house before I lose my nerve. There are half a dozen cars in the driveway, and I pull in behind the last one. I can hear the soft thump of music playing from the backyard as I walk up to the pristine white steps in front of her house.

I ring the doorbell and wait.

An older woman dressed in a blue gown answers the door. "Hello there," she says with a pleasant twang in her voice. "May I help you?"

"I'm here to see Maddie," I say, my throat feeling dry. "I know you're having a wedding tonight, so maybe she could just meet me out here?"

"Nonsense," the woman says, waving at me to come in. "Wait, you are Colby, right?"

I nod. Who is this woman and how does she know my name? Surely, that's a good sign.

"The wedding is over and everyone is enjoying the reception now," she says, leading me through a marble foyer. "You're just in time for the fun."

I try to smile, but it probably makes me look like an idiot. I'm taken through the house and to the backyard, where the patio has been turned into a sparkling white, flower-decorated wedding reception. A live band plays in the corner, and well-dressed people are dancing and having fun.

"There she is," the woman says, pointing on the dance floor. I see Maddie looking like a princess in a purple dress that goes down to the floor. She's dancing while holding the hands of a little girl around five years old. Her smile sparkles under the twinkling lights, and she looks so happy I immediately regret coming here. I regret everything, all of it.

And then she looks at me.

35

MADDIE

EMMA'S HAND slips from my grip as I stand up. She turns, following my gaze to the unexpected visitor who just appeared on the patio.

"Is that Colby?" she says. Before I answer, she breaks into a smile and waves at him, her chubby hand wobbling back and forth.

"Yes," I say, but my heart is pounding so hard I can't really hear myself talk. "I'll be right back," I tell her.

"Can I come, too?" she asks. I stop, turning and bending down to her eye level.

"Let me talk to him first, okay? And then maybe you can come talk to him in a little bit."

She looks past me at Colby, considering it for a second. "Okay."

I smile and give her a little hug. To anyone else, I look like I'm comforting a kid, but in reality, I'm comforting myself. Too bad her tiny little hug doesn't help much. The pain in my chest is far too big to be bandaged by a five-year-old.

I swallow the lump in my throat, take a deep breath, and walk to Colby. On the dance floor behind me, my mom and Landon are wrapped in each other, swaying to the music. My aunt and uncle are dancing a few feet away, and our friends and relatives are all absorbed in their own lives, oblivious that I might be walking straight toward my doom.

At least he's dressed well, if this is the last time I'll ever talk to him.

I stop just a few feet in front of him. We're standing under the covered part of our large backyard patio. There's a string of clear lights hanging overhead, the dip in the strand hovering just a couple inches above Colby's head.

I open my mouth to say something lame like *hey* or *hi*, but nothing comes out.

"Can we go somewhere to talk?" Colby asks. He adjusts the lapel of his jacket. "Just for a second."

"If it's only a second, why can't you say it here?" I ask. Ugh, I'm not trying to be difficult, but, well I don't know what I'm being. This is hard. It hurts looking at him, especially when he looks so remarkably sexy in that suit.

"Please, Maddie?"

Hearing him say my name makes me weak in the knees. I let out a breath and start walking toward the house. "Come on," I say, not looking back to make sure he's following.

We slip inside, past the kitchen, which is busy with half a dozen caterers mulling around. I could take him to my room, but that's too intimate for a final breakup talk, so instead I turn right and slip into the laundry room. It's as big as our old living room used to be, so there's plenty of room to talk.

Colby brushes by me, smelling like clean boy with the

smallest scent of peppermint. I clench my jaw and close the door, locking it.

Then I turn around. "What is it, Colby?" I toss my hands up in the universal gesture for defeat. "There's nothing you can say that will make me feel worse, okay? I swear, I've suffered enough for what I did to you."

"I'm not here to berate you, Maddie."

Colby's fingers twist together, his shoulders slumped, long hair starting to fall apart in pieces that he'd brushed back. "Then what is it?" I say, taking a step backward. My hands touch the washing machine, and I hold onto it for support. Being this close to him makes me want to collapse and cry. Even in my daydreams, he wasn't this handsome. God, why did he have to wear a suit that looks so hot on him? Why can't he just go away and let me be miserable by myself?

"Mindy told me everything you told her," he says, stepping forward. My feet shuffle back, but there's nowhere to go, the cold metal of the washing machine door pressing against my calves.

"I understand why you did it," he says, his eyes burning a hole into me even though I'm staring at the floor, at the little blue chevron patterns in the rug beneath our feet.

I don't say anything. How can I? I lied to him about who I am, who I was. And the worst part? I would have let it go on as long as possible just to save myself the embarrassment of the truth.

"I'm sorry, for what it's worth," I finally say, not meeting his eyes.

"Maddie, look at me," Colby says. He's just a few inches

away now. I could look up and lean forward and I'd probably be touching him. Instead, I keep my eyes on my shoes.

"I said I'm sorry, Colby. I really don't have anything else to say."

"Why not?" His voice rises an octave and he takes a step back. "You told Mindy everything, but you can't tell me anything at all? Why? You two are just friends and I'm your *boyfriend*, Maddie. Talk to me."

I look up now, the B-word searing into my heart like a hot dagger. "You know how Mindy is," I say, pressing my lips together. "She made me tell her even though I didn't want to."

His lips twist into a slight grin, his head tilting slightly. "I wish I had as much power as Mindy. I wish you would talk to me."

"What is there to talk about?" I heave a resigned sigh. As much as I love looking at this boy, as much as his honeyed voice makes my toes tingle, now I just want to leave and be alone. I can't stand being right next to someone I can't have.

I stand a little straighter. "I'm trailer trash, Colby. I'm a poor, trash, *loser* who happened to luck out when my mom met a rich guy. I'll never be one of the typical girls you date in high school. I'm just like them. I can't be, no matter how rich and popular I suddenly get, that's not me."

Colby moves closer, his hands grabbing my arms, his eyes boring into mine. "That's why I love you, Maddie. I love that you're not like the other girls. I don't want one of them. I'm *sick* of typical. I want you."

"I—" I can't say it. The words won't come for the longest time, and we just stand here, his hands gripping me tightly but not painfully, his face an expression of desperation. "You should hate me. I lied to you."

He laughs, a snort at first, but then it turns into full out laughter. He drags his hands down his face and then sweeps them through his hair. "Maybe I should hate you. But I can't. I am completely in love with you."

My heart pounds loudly in my ears. My fingers tingle and I am suddenly so very sure that I've slipped and hit my head and now I'm daydreaming all of this. "I lied to you," I say, my voice barely above a whisper.

"About stupid things, right? I mean, our talks, our inside jokes . . . our epic make out sessions . . ." He lifts an eyebrow. "That was real, right? The girl you were when you were with me, tell me that was real? Because nothing else matters but that."

I blink and tears roll down my cheek. "It was real, but—"

He shakes his head, taking my hands in his. "That's all that matters. I'm sorry I didn't notice you before, Maddie. I should have. I should have seen you the day you first moved here and then we could have been dating a lot longer." He squeezes my hands, inching forward until our toes touch, his forehead tilting to press against mine. "Please forgive me for taking so long to see you."

"I'm the one who needs forgiving, not you."

"Let's both forgive each other at the same time." Colby lifts an eyebrow, a devilish grin making my toes tingle.

I chuckle. "Okay. On three."

"One," he says. "Two . . . three."

I grin, not sure what we're supposed to do now. But then I'm lifted off my feet, twirled through the air, and set back down again. Colby's lips press against mine, his hands holding me tightly.

This kiss is just like the first one: nervous and passionate, a little scared but full of possibility. When he pulls away, I realize a steady stream of tears have been slipping down my cheeks, a mixture of pain and love and hope of what's yet to come.

Colby brushes away the tears, his thumbs soft and gentle on my face.

"What do we do now? I ask, peering up into his brown eyes.

He holds out a hand in a sweeping gesture. "How about a dance?"

36

JOSH

GRADUATING high school was supposed to feel like becoming an adult. After so many years of slogging through early morning alarms, bumpy bus rides, and crappy cafeteria food, the day after graduation was supposed to be . . . different. Guess I thought I'd feel like an official adult or something.

Besides the fact that I slept until noon, my life feels exactly the same. Some seniors from my school are planning to move across the country and become crazy party college freshman, but not me. I'm just stuck here in Louetta, Texas, a small town with a few good pizza joints, but nothing really exciting to brag about. I'll be starting good ol' community college in the fall, for what, I have no idea. Mom said she'd help me sign up for core classes. Dad said I'll have a blast. I'm not exactly sure how true that is, since I've seen the campus and it looks like a combination of a thrift store and like, an old Walmart. Once college starts, I'll have two years to figure out what I'd like to major in, and then maybe, I'll feel more like an adult.

Right now I'm just happy to have one last summer of not doing a thing except working at the family business, The Flying Mermaid. It's a surf shop on the beach, passed down from my grandparents. It was a TV repair shop when they owned it. My parents turned it into a surf shop with a little section at the front for gifts and girly crap my mom loves. It's a pretty popular hangout at Blue Beach, and working there has always felt more like fun than actual work.

Of course, there are other things I aspire to do this summer. Like get a girlfriend.

I know, I know. *What the hell is wrong with you, Josh Graham?* I spent most of my senior year swearing off dating because it never works out. After Elise broke my heart—the third girl in four years to do such a thing—I swore off girls. Not forever, but for a while. Having your heart ripped to shreds a few times will do that to you. It's not like I'm some crybaby loser about it or anything, but it still sucks.

My no dating self-promise didn't exactly last very long, because I've been checking my dating app more times than I'd ever admit out loud. I guess I keep hoping I'll refresh the stupid thing and see that I've matched with a girl who is perfect for me. My soul mate, found on a dating app.

Right, because that's how real love stories all start. Ugh.

I run my finger along the Xbox games on Colby's shelf. "Can I borrow this one?" I ask, pulling out a game. My best friend's bedroom is like a video game utopia since he's kept every console he's ever had.

"Sure," he says, not even looking at it. He's going through his drawers, tossing clothes into an open suitcase on his bed.

I turn back to the games. "What about this one and this one?"

"Take whatever you want," he says, holding up a blue T-shirt and curling his lip as he decides to take it or not. "I trust you won't bring them back scratched and covered in dried soda like that idiot Bryce did to my Assassin's Creed."

"Obviously," I say, grabbing a few more. "I respect other people's stuff."

I'm over here at my best friend's house to see him off on his glamorous summer vacation. I wouldn't normally borrow so many games at once, but I'm going to be bored without him this summer.

He's only been dating Maddie for a couple of months, but her step-dad is loaded and he's taking them all to his vacation home in Madrid for the month.

Yeah, Madrid, *Spain.*

And it's not that I'm jealous. I mean yeah, Maddie is adorable and all, but she's totally his type of girl, and I don't *have* to have a girlfriend whose family comes with those kinds of benefits or anything—but it would be nice.

Not the vacation home in Spain. (Not that I'd turn an invite like that down.) The family. Colby and Maddie's family get along really well. She has a couple of sisters and they adore him, and her parents adore him, and they're always hanging out and having a blast. I guess that's the part that makes me jealous.

Not only did my best friend land the perfect girl for him,

but he found a whole new family. My last three girlfriends all hated my little sister, Abigail. Sure, she's a kid and she's annoying, but she's thirteen now so I'd like to have the big family happiness thing like Colby has. So although I'd sworn off dating and had pretty much convinced myself I was happy about it, now I want a girlfriend.

Bad.

I want the friendship and love and even the stupid girly things they like to do, like date nights and sappy nicknames. I want to be in love again, but this time I don't want my heart shredded. I don't want to be lied to, or cheated on, or used. I never even saw it coming with Elise.

We'd been together over a year, happily—or, at least I thought we were happy. I was sneakily trying to figure out if she'd prefer white gold or yellow gold for this necklace I was going to buy her for her birthday. Her little sister let me inside when Elise was supposed to be at softball practice, and I snuck into her room to look at her jewelry box. The plan was to examine her jewelry and get a feel for what she'd prefer. The moment I stepped into her room, my plans were shattered. Instead of finding her jewelry box, I found her sitting on some guy's lap while he fumbled with her bra strap.

The worst part was she didn't even seem ashamed about it. She'd told me we should have broken up a long time ago. That I should have seen it coming. That, *didn't I feel the same way, too?*

Uh no, I didn't. To this day, I'm not sure if she really meant it, that she thought we both wanted to break up, or if she was just lying. Because in my mind, our relationship was great. We had fun and we loved each other, and we were in the popular crowd at high school. What more could we have wanted?

I swallow the lump in my throat and hold the stack of video games under my arm.

"So I'm guessing everyone speaks Spanish in Madrid, huh?" I ask.

Colby nods. "That's why Mads and I have been taking Spanish lessons. She's way better than I am."

"You excited?"

He looks up, a crooked grin on his face. "I mean, her parents are going to be there, so it won't be some romantic trip or anything, but yeah. It's Madrid. I'm psyched."

I draw in a deep breath and let it out slowly. "Hey man, at least one of us is happy."

"You'll get there," he says, rolling his eyes. "Of course, I thought you were against girlfriends? Didn't your mom convince you that all young relationships are pointless?"

I nod. "Yeah, but she was probably saying that to make me feel better about Elise."

He laughs. "Do what you gotta do, man. If you want a girlfriend, go get one."

I hold up my phone. "That's what I've been trying to do."

Colby lifts an eyebrow. "Please tell me you're not using that dating app again? That thing is disgusting. Nothing but weirdos on there."

I shrug. "Where else am I going to find girls?"

Colby gives me a stare like I'm an idiot, and I mean, yeah I guess I am. "You find them in real life, you dipshit. Go *outside*. Meet girls."

I nod, running a hand through my hair. "That's what I'll do after my date with Jenny."

"Jenny?"

I open the app and scroll to this girl's profile. There's not much on there, and only one picture of her face, but she's pretty enough. She practically begged me to go out with her after we chatted through the app a few minutes. So far she seems kind of boring, or at least not very good at chatting online, but maybe an in-person date will fix that.

I figured going on this one date can't possibly hurt, and maybe it'll lead to something good. I turn my phone around and show it to Colby.

His brows pull together while he examines her photo. "Eh."

"Oh, come on. She's cute," I say, looking at the picture again. "It's just one date. If it doesn't work out, then I'll take your advice and go outside."

He closes his suitcase and zips it. "I think you should go outside regardless, man. I literally met Maddie outside."

"I'll be spending my summer at the Flying Mermaid," I say, sliding my phone back in my pocket. "If things with this girl don't work out, I'll be spending plenty of time outside since the shop is halfway on the sand."

"With chicks in bikinis," he says, fist-bumping me. "Nice."

I snort. When I was younger, I loved being at the beach for that reason. But after spending every summer of my life working at the surf shop, one bikini blends into another one and it kind of gets old. Unlike our friend Bryce, checking out hot girls isn't the only thing on my agenda.

I'd like to find a real girlfriend. The kind Colby has, and the kind I've always wanted. Maybe this Jenny girl will fit the bill. If not, I guess I'll have to keep looking.

37

___

BESS

THE SMELL of maple syrup wakes me up on the first day of summer break. It's not a bad way to wake up, that's for sure. Grandma is an amazing cook, but during the school year I'm usually eating Pop-Tarts or cereal on my mad dash out the door. I'm not the kind of girl who wakes up two hours early to shower and fix my hair, and put on a ton of makeup with fifty different applicator brushes.

Don't get me wrong—I'd love to be that kind of girl.

But look at me. Ew. There's no point in "putting makeup on a pig" as this guy Bryce used to say in junior high. I remember the day clearly, the same way I remember just about every instance of being bullied. It was the first day back to eighth grade after the Christmas break, and Grandma had given me a makeup set for Christmas. I was in love. It was the good kind, from Sephora, this fancy makeup place in the mall. Until then, I'd only amassed a collection of drugstore lip gloss and some cheap powder that promised to eliminate shine. (Spoiler alert: it did not.)

I'd been spending a ton of time online looking up makeup tutorials, and I guess that's what gave Grandma the idea. I was so excited, I spent forty-five minutes just on my eyeliner. Things were looking up for me. I'd lost ten pounds since school started, and now I had beautiful makeup.

And then, of course, Bryce ruined it all by calling me a pig. He said it in front of everyone in the cafeteria. Grandma had tried to comfort me by saying some of the students were probably doing their own thing and didn't notice him say it, but it didn't help much. Because I know he said it, and all of his friends laughed. Even one person knowing my humiliation was enough to ruin the rest of the year for me. It didn't take long for me to gain back those ten pounds, and then about five more.

I put that makeup in my drawer and didn't touch it again until freshman year when Grandma and I went out to celebrate her sixty-third birthday. She wanted to go to this Thai restaurant two towns over, so I figured I was safe from the prying eyes of my peers. I'd felt pretty that night. I haven't felt that way since.

My mouth waters at the smell of breakfast rising up from the kitchen. As much as I want to stay in bed and begin my uber lazy summer of doing absolutely nothing until college classes start in August, it would be rude to make Grandma cook all by herself. The woman is my rock. She took over raising me when my teenaged parents moved out. Unlike most fifteen-year-old parents, mine actually loved each other and wanted to stay together. As far as I know, they still are together. They just didn't think having a kid fit in well with their traveling-the-world-with-a-backpack scene, so they left me with Grandma. She's somehow managed to be a mother, father, and both grandparents to me for my whole life. Her husband, my Grandad, died just a few months before I was born. She said I gave her back the life that was taken away from her.

So yeah, there's no way I can make that woman cook breakfast all by herself. She's far too important to me.

I crawl out of bed and climb over the mess of craft supplies I'd left on the floor last night. Although I consider myself a neat person, my room is kind of a disaster area right now. My dream is to become a kindergarten teacher, and although graduation is still four years away, I'm kind of obsessed with craft ideas for my future classroom. Plus, my cousin Aisha is a teacher and she said that coming up with creative teaching tools and crafts for the kids always gave you bonus points with the professors, so that's what I plan on doing. Right now, I'm deep in the middle of about four Pinterest projects I found for kindergarten lesson plans. I'm having a blast, and I haven't even started teaching kids yet.

I slip into the hallway, past the empty cat bed in the alcove near the stairs. My heart aches as I blow a little kiss toward the bed. My cat, Missy, died a few months ago. She'd been with me for as long as I could remember, my little calico furball of a best friend. But old age got to her eventually, and we buried her in the backyard. I haven't found it in me to move the cat bed. Every time I walk past it, I can almost pretend she's just snoozing in the other room and that she'll be back any minute.

"Good morning," I say, meeting Grandma in the kitchen. Though she works at an insurance company, I've always thought she would make an excellent chef. She has a way with food, and I'm not just saying that because I'm fat and love food.

"Morning, hun," Grandma says, flashing me a smile that is all white teeth and red lipstick. Even though it's Saturday, you'd think she's going to work with how nicely she's dressed. My grandmother is the opposite of me in that way. I'm all pajamas and T-shirts, she's all silk blouses and dress pants.

"Can I help with anything?" I ask, opening the cabinet to grab plates to set the table.

"No, I have it all covered." Grandma takes the plates from me and goes over to the table, setting them down in our usual spots. "Why don't you make yourself a cup of coffee? Breakfast will be ready in a second. I made your favorites: French toast, bacon, sausage, scrambled eggs, and thinly sliced toast with butter."

"That's a lot of food," I say, frowning. Usually we'll have French toast *or* eggs and bacon, never both at the same time. I make some coffee and sit at the table. "I was actually thinking I might try to diet this summer so I can start out college as less of a fat cow."

Grandma puts a hand on her hip. "You are not a fat cow!"

I take a sip of coffee. "It's literally in my name, Grandma. Bess. Short for Bessie, as in Bessie the cow."

"That is not what you're named after," she says, rolling her eyes as she piles several slices of French toast onto a plate that she puts in the center of the table.

I've been called Bessie the cow since I was five. It wasn't until around the age of seven that I got smart enough to shorten my name to Bess. Now that particular insult comes less frequently.

I rest my chin in my hand. "We don't really know what I'm named after, now do we?"

I heave a sigh and Grandma frowns, but she doesn't say anything. My mother named me "Bessie" on my birth certificate, but then she never explained what gave her the idea. Maybe she knew I'd be a fat cow when I got older and she was just preparing me for it.

Grandma joins me at the table and we start filling our plates from the massive breakfast feast she's prepared. "You didn't have to do all of this," I say, reaching for another piece of sausage. Then it hits me. I look up and fix her with an accusing glare. "Wait, why did you make all of this food?"

Grandma dunks a piece of French toast in syrup and gives me this apathetic look. "I don't think you need to diet, Bess. That's just asking for stress, and stress makes you way unhealthier than a little extra weight."

I lift an eyebrow. "You didn't answer my question."

Grandma is a large woman. She's been round and happy about it for as long as I remember. She's the kind of lady who is unabashedly in love with food and doesn't let someone's perceptions of what's attractive or not stand in her way. Unfortunately, I inherited her love of food, but not her love of being happy with your own body.

I hate my body.

I point my fork at her. "Why are you buttering me up?"

She waves a hand at me. "You're being silly. I just wanted a nice breakfast since school is over. It's to congratulate you on graduating, honey."

I snort. "Just yesterday you said graduating high school was the easiest part of life and that no one should bother having a party for something so easy."

"I was being facetious," she says with a little roll of her hand. "Of course we should celebrate."

"I'm still not entirely convinced that this breakfast isn't some kind of bribe," I say, going back to eating.

"So anyway, what are you planning to do this summer?" she asks, her voice light.

"Not a single thing," I say with a smile. "College will be hard, so I want to take it easy."

"Or—" she says, giving me this wide-eyed look like she just thought of the idea. "You could help out my dear friend Julie. She gets so busy during the summers and it's so hard running that shop by herself . . ."

I shake my head. Grandma's friend Julie owns this little boutique on the beach that sells overpriced (but cute) trinkets, clothing, baby stuff, and gifts.

"Not happening. That place is full of rich annoying people."

"Julie's not rich or annoying," Grandma says, as if she's making some kind of point here.

"I don't really need a job," I say, reaching for the jar of honey on the table. "Mom and Dad sent me more money a few days ago."

My parents have been traveling my entire life, but they show their love, or whatever they want to call it, by sending me checks in the mail every so often. Sometimes they come once a month, sometimes a year or two will pass between the checks. I always get a birthday card and a Christmas gift, though. Recently, I received a check for five thousand dollars in an envelope that simply had a Post-It note stuck to the check. "Love you" was scrawled on it in handwriting that I'm not sure is Mom's or Dad's. Their checks still have Grandma's address on them, even though they haven't lived here since I was born. The life of a nomad is a strange thing, and I don't pretend to understand it.

"It's not exactly about the money," Grandma says. She rolls her bottom lip under her teeth and gives me this shaky smile. "I kind of already told her you'd love to work there."

"You what!" I drop my fork and it clangs to the plate, making this awful sound that grates on my nerves. "I don't want to work at the beach, Grandma! There's nothing but skinny jerks there!"

She gives me a look. "There are skinny people everywhere, kid. There's also fat people, and tall people, and short people."

I sigh. "I don't care about *those* people. I only care about the women who are beautiful and stunning and make me feel like a total loser."

Grandma snorts. "You are being silly. Julie really needs you. You can refuse her if you want, I guess, but it'd be good karma if you just get over your insecurities and go help her out for the summer."

"I can't just get over it," I say, shaking my head as I stare at my food. Suddenly, and probably for the first time in my life, I am not hungry. "You don't understand," I say. "There will be girls I know from school there."

"Bess, I wish you'd realize you're a beautiful girl," Grandma says. "Your weight is not an indicator of that.

Working at the shop is just a job. You'll probably be behind the counter the whole time. In that case, who cares? You're not going on a date here, or joining some reality TV show beauty contest for God's sake."

I bite the inside of my lip. I guess she's right about that. I can't hide out in my room forever, as much as that might sound like a nice idea.

Besides, I *did* hope to go on a diet this summer. Maybe being at the store will keep me on my feet and give me more exercise. I could pack healthy snacks for the day, that way I can't go into our pantry all day and eat junk. This could work, I guess.

"Fine, I'll take the stupid job," I mutter, focusing on my fork instead of my grandmother.

She reaches across the table and pats my hand. "You'll be okay, sweetie. I promise."

ABOUT THE AUTHOR

Amy Sparling is the bestselling author of books for teens and the teens at heart. She lives on the coast of Texas with her family, her spoiled rotten pets, and a huge pile of books. She graduated with a degree in English and has worked at a bookstore, coffee shop, and a fashion boutique. Her fashion skills aren't the best, but luckily she turned her love of coffee and books into a writing career that means she can work in her pajamas. Her favorite things are coffee, book boyfriends, and Netflix binges.

She's always loved reading books from R. L. Stine's Fear Street series, to The Baby Sitter's Club series by Ann, Martin, and of course, Twilight. She started writing her own books in 2010 and now publishes several books a year. Amy loves getting messages from her readers and responds to every single one! Connect with her on one of the links below.

Website: AmySparling.com
Instagram: @writeamysparling
Goodreads: goodreads.com/Amy_Sparling
Wattpad: AmySparlingWrites